"This is an excellent boo. tive really draws you into the action and tension of the story and, importantly, excites your curiosity to read the pages of the Bible itself. My own kids will love reading this, and it will prompt some good discussions about God's anointed King."

MIKE DICKER, Principal, Youthworks College, New South Wales, Australia

"The Bible tells us that God works through living, breathing, real people. Katy brings to life an extraordinary biblical story of some of those people and how they laugh and cry and dance and fight so that young people feel the power of God to work in our ordinary lives to achieve his amazing purposes."

ED DREW, Founder, Faith in Kids; Author, *Raising Confident Kids in a Confusing World*

"A super book by a gifted writer, this wonderful retelling of a Bible story gets under the skins of Saul, Jonathan, David and lots of other characters, during some of the most emotional and dramatic scenes in Israel's history. While staying faithful to the Bible plotline, Katy Morgan draws out the hopes, the fears, the belief and the unbelief all used by God to bring David to the throne. Skilfully, she draws us into the story so that we turn the pages eager to read what happens next. Best of all, she whets the appetite to read the story in the Bible itself. Don't miss out the Epilogue!"

CHRISTOPHER ASH, Writer-in-Residence, Tyndale House, Cambridge

"Far too many people believe the Old Testament is largely irrelevant. Katy Morgan shows us that it is bursting with promise, feasting and song. Her vivid writing, combined with her deep knowledge of the ancient world, plunges us into this unfolding drama. The heartbeat of this book is a longing for its readers to find confidence in the then-coming-now-arrived King of Israel. Katy is a gifted storyteller— the pacing will keep younger readers engaged while the detail will help older readers reflect. There's food for all of us, and the Notes section is a must for those who want the recipe."

NATE MORGAN-LOCKE, Creative Director,
SpeakLife; Film-maker; Author

THE SONGS OF A WARRIOR

SAUL AND DAVID: A RETELLING

KATY MORGAN

Katy Morgan is the author of *The Promise and the Light,* and an Editor at The Good Book Company. She likes climbing hills and exploring new places—both in books and in real life! Before Katy joined TGBC she used to work in a school, and now she teaches the Bible every week to children at her church. She also reads ancient Greek and has a master's degree in Classics from Cambridge University.

The Songs of a Warrior
© The Good Book Company, 2023. Reprinted 2024.

Published by:
The Good Book Company

thegoodbook.com | thegoodbook.co.uk
thegoodbook.com.au | thegoodbook.co.nz | thegoodbook.co.in

Cover illustration by Megan Parker | Internal illustrations by Alex Webb-Peploe
Design and Art Direction by André Parker

ISBN: 9781784988173 | JOB-007699 | Printed in the UK

Contents

The map on the right is full of real places, because the story you're about to read is based on a true one, found in the Old Testament part of the Bible. If you find yourself wanting to know more about the history that lies behind this book, turn to page 253—there are accompanying notes for each chapter.

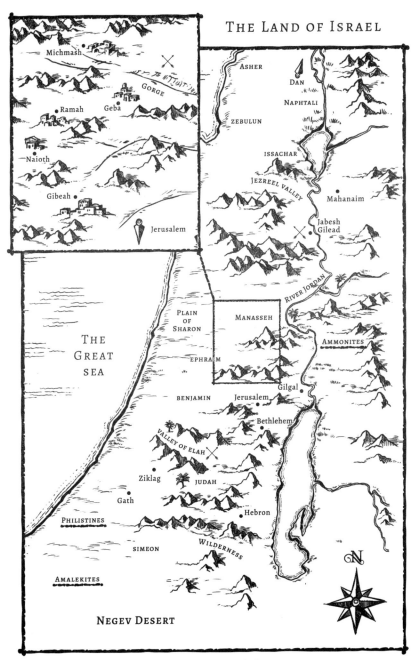

THE LAND OF ISRAEL

ASHER

DAN

NAPHTALI

ZEBULUN

Michmash

GORGE

Ramah

Geba

ISSACHAR

Naioth

JEZREEL VALLEY

Mahanaim

Gibeah

Jabesh
Gilead

Jerusalem

RIVER JORDAN

PLAIN
OF
SHARON

MANASSEH

THE
GREAT
SEA

EPHRAIM

AMMONITES

BENJAMIN

Jerusalem

Gilgal

Bethlehem

VALLEY OF ELAH

Ziklag

JUDAH

Gath

Hebron

PHILISTINES

SIMEON

WILDERNESS

N

AMALEKITES

NEGEV DESERT

● Town/City   ✕ Site of battle   ⚊•⚊ Foreign tribe

Cast of Characters

THE HOUSE OF KISH

Kish, a wealthy farmer
Saul, Kish's son
Abner, Saul's cousin
Jonathan and Ishvi, the sons of Saul
Michal and Merab, the daughters of Saul

THE HOUSE OF JESSE

Jesse, a sheep-farmer
David, the eighth son of Jesse
Eliab and Abinadab, two of David's brothers
Zeruiah, David's sister
Joab, Abishai and Asahel, the sons of Zeruiah

OTHERS IN ISRAEL

Samuel, a prophet
Nathan, a prophet
Abiathar, a priest
Oren, a shepherd (invented character)
Noa, a servant (invented character)
Maoz, a bad man (invented character)
Ahimelek, a Hittite

PHILISTINES

Goliath, a warrior
Achish, the king of Gath

The God of Israel spoke,
   the Rock of Israel said to me:
"When one rules over people in righteousness,
   when he rules in the fear of God,
he is like the light of morning at sunrise
   on a cloudless morning,
like the brightness after rain
   that brings grass from the earth."

2 Samuel chapter 23, verses 3-4

PART ONE

A King for All Israel

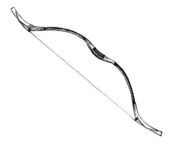

CHAPTER 1

The Boy with the Bow

There was a rock-dove in the tree. It was plump and purplish and looking happily away into the distance.

The boy on the ground beneath it was slowly raising his bow and carefully sliding an arrow out of his quiver.

Gently, Jonathan, he told himself, keeping his eyes fixed on the dove. He did feel a little sorry for it as it ruffled its feathers in a self-satisfied sort of way and clicked its beak. Poor silly bird. At least its last hour had been a happy one.

The arrow was out. He notched its feathered end to the bowstring.

Jonathan had made this bow himself, and it was a good one. It was small, just a hunting bow, not as big as the ones you'd use in battle. He had been practising with his grandfather's old war-bow but he couldn't bend it far enough to shoot it—not yet. But this one was just right.

His feet were firm. His hands were steady. He closed one eye and drew the arrow back…

Then, suddenly, the moment was lost. Somewhere behind Jonathan a sheep bleated. All at once the rock-dove panicked and took off in a flurry of feathers.

Not its last hour, after all.

Jonathan groaned. Where had a *sheep* appeared from? Now he would have to go home empty-handed!

He turned round. There were three of them, all craggy old ewes with soft muzzles and dirty fleeces. They looked at him indignantly as if he had no right to be there.

Jonathan looked at them back. "You're in *my* way, I'm not in yours," he said.

He wondered who they belonged to. It would be odd to bring sheep into the woods deliberately. Had they got lost? They must have come up the hill… He'd better chase them back that way.

He had time. His grandfather Kish had said they had to leave for Mizpah at noon, and judging by the sun he wasn't late yet.

His stomach squirmed. Today was the day! He'd been looking forward to the assembly at Mizpah for weeks. And now, at last, the day had come when—

But Jonathan's thoughts were interrupted by a shout. Someone was calling out for help. Someone at the bottom of the hill, beyond the edge of the wood.

Without hesitating, Jonathan ran at the sheep, waving his bow in the air. "Yah!"

They jerked back, then lowered their heads and thundered away downhill. One of them almost got caught by the lower branches of a thorn tree, but she shook herself loose and followed her companions.

Jonathan followed too. His eyes took a moment to adjust to the sunlight as he left the wood, but soon he was watching the sheep race down to the valley-bottom—and there was the boy who'd shouted. He was still shouting, and waving frantically. He was about Jonathan's age and he had two more sheep at his heels.

What had happened? Jonathan set off running down the hill, sending small rocks tumbling as he did. He jumped from side to side to avoid them, took on speed, skidded down the last steep slope, and arrived at the bottom with a heaving chest and a wide grin on his face. He liked running.

But the shepherd boy wasn't smiling. "Did you see them?" he said urgently. "Did you see where they went?"

"Who? The sheep?"

"The thieves." The boy's dirty face was streaked with tears. "My master will kill me—they're all gone—some men came and took them—I couldn't stop them—but I can't go home with just five sheep—"

"Don't worry," Jonathan interrupted gently. "Those three were up in the wood. Maybe others will have escaped as well. Is this the direction the thieves came in?

How long ago did they take them?"

"Not too long. Maybe half an hour ago." The boy was calming down. He focused on Jonathan, grasping his arm. "You're Kish's grandson, aren't you? Can you help me? I'm Oren. I'm only a shepherd but—" His eyes were pleading and eager.

"I'll help," Jonathan said. Then he hesitated, glancing up at the sky. "But I've got to go soon. We're going to Mizpah."

"To the assembly!" Oren's eyes widened. "Then you'd better not help me. You can't be late for that. Not when…"

It was too huge a thing to say out loud. But Jonathan finished the other boy's sentence in his own head. *Not when God is going to choose a king for us.*

He looked at the sky again. It wasn't noon yet. "I have time," he decided. "A bit, anyway."

Oren nodded, suddenly becoming businesslike. "If I keep these five together, will you run ahead? Look for the others? You're a good runner."

Jonathan grinned—and sprinted away at full speed. His sandals left clouds of dust behind him.

But he didn't find any of the other sheep.

"Maybe they'll just wander home," he told Oren encouragingly as the two of them trailed back towards the town. "Some of our donkeys went missing a couple of months ago, and *they* returned."

"But your donkeys weren't stolen, were they?" said

Oren gloomily. "They just got loose. I heard about it."
He kicked at the dust.

Briefly Jonathan wondered what Oren had heard
about the donkeys. His father, Saul, had gone to find
them, but they'd wandered back while he was gone. Kish
had raged, "That useless son of mine! He's probably
halfway to Jabesh Gilead by now, and all the time the
stupid donkeys were under his nose!"

Jonathan's cheeks went pink as he remembered. It
wasn't a good feeling, thinking your father might be
useless.

"My master will kill me," said Oren. "He hits me
when I mess up just *small* things."

At that Jonathan forgot his father and grandfather.
He wished he and Oren had been able to find the
sheep. Fiercely, he said, "This is why we need a king.
He'd stop people stealing and—and people beating up
their servants."

"Maybe," replied Oren dully.

They'd reached the edge of Gibeah. Jonathan squeezed
Oren on the arm, and the other boy trudged disconso-
lately away.

Jonathan followed the opposite path, looping around
the low flat hill that supported the main part of the
town. In front of him lay his grandfather's fields: they
were bare and brown at the moment, ready for ploughing. Then there was the house, and the green rolling
hills, with Kish's sheep grazing on them. Jonathan

smiled contentedly as the sun found its way through a crack in the clouds and filled the valley with brilliant colour.

Then he gasped, and broke into a run. The sun! It was past noon! He was going to be late.

He got away with just a raised eyebrow from Kish, who was standing impressively outside the house, his arms folded over his thick sheepskin coat. Abner was next to him, equally broad-chested but brown-haired instead of grey. Abner was Saul's cousin, Kish's nephew.

Jonathan's father, Saul, came out of the house. His tall frame was swaddled in a cloak, the richest one he had. There was fur sewn round its neck. He had put oil in his hair and rings on his fingers. "Jonathan," he exclaimed, "you're here at last." His eyes slid uncertainly to Kish. "You're late."

Kish said nothing, so Saul didn't say anything else either. A servant came round the house with the donkeys, and Jonathan hurried inside to get changed. He had to wear a heavy coat like his grandfather's, which he could already tell was going to be itchy and too hot. He had an embroidered cap over his hair and proper boots instead of sandals. His sister Merab handed him a thin gold ring: "Grandfather told me to give it to you. Now that you're one of the men."

Her voice was sarcastic, but Jonathan ignored that.

She was right: he was one of the men now, going with his father and grandfather to represent their family and clan and tribe at the great gathering of all Israel. Right now it was the house of Kish, and then it would be the house of Saul, but one day people would talk about the house of Jonathan, who was not only an excellent hunter but also owned hundreds of sheep, and treated all his shepherds with respect.

Or, he thought excitedly, *Jonathan, the right-hand man of the king, the king God chose, the one who rules over all twelve tribes of Israel.*

He slid the ring onto his finger. It was too big, but he didn't let Merab see.

Outside again, the donkeys had been spread with fine fabrics and leather saddlebags. Mizpah was close enough that they could have walked there, but that would have looked cheap and unimpressive. They were going to take donkeys, and five servants, and everyone would know that the house of Kish was one of the best families in the whole tribe of Benjamin.

Michal, Jonathan's other sister, had twined herself around Saul's arm. "When will you be back?" she asked. "You were gone for ages and ages last time."

Saul shook her off. "Soon," he said, and climbed onto his donkey.

Michal transferred herself to Jonathan. She was six years younger than him and much skinnier; her bony arms clung tightly around his waist.

Jonathan squeezed her back. "See you later," he whispered, bending to touch the top of her head with his chin. "I can't wait to tell you all about it."

Her dark head nodded, and she stood back, letting him get onto his donkey.

"Ready?" growled Kish.

"Let's go," answered Saul.

CHAPTER 2

The Stone of Help

Jonathan didn't travel by donkey very often. The journey to Mizpah was easy in comparison to all the haring around he'd done that morning. Lazily, he sank back against his saddlebag and said, to no one in particular, "It's good we don't have to go very far. I wonder why the assembly is in Mizpah."

"Because that's where Samuel chose," said Abner shortly, "and he's the prophet. God probably told him it had to be in Mizpah."

Abner's tone of voice did not invite any more questions, but Jonathan's curiosity remained un-dampened. "Can Samuel really hear God speak?" he asked. "Actually hear him?"

"That's what they say."

"What's he like?" Jonathan twisted round and looked at his father, who was bringing up the rear. "You've met him. You haven't really told us what he was like."

Saul's face was unreadable. "Old," he said non-com-mittally. "I think… I think he does hear God speak, yes."

"How do you know?" Jonathan knew that his father had met Samuel when he'd been off looking for the don-keys, but he'd been told nothing else about the encoun-ter. Saul had been resistant to questioning. But now, maybe… "Did he speak God's words to *you*?" Jonathan asked excitedly.

It was the obvious question to ask, but Saul seemed a bit taken aback by it. He blinked and pressed his lips together. Eventually he said, "He told me the donkeys had been found."

Jonathan turned forwards again disappointedly. That didn't seem like a very impressive thing to tell anyone. Wasn't God concerned with bigger things than a few donkeys?

Kish, in front, seemed to read Jonathan's mind. "Don't turn your nose up at that," he said. "A God who helps us with what we need—that's a God I'm glad to worship."

Jonathan knew where his grandfather's thoughts were leading. "And we need a king," he said.

"Yes," answered Kish. "A king to lead us in battle—all twelve tribes—and solve our disputes. That's what we've been missing."

Jonathan considered this. He thought about Oren and his master who beat him up: *could* a king stop things like that happening? Then he said, "Which tribe do you think the king will come from? Judah, maybe, they're one of the biggest. Or Manasseh—"

"Only the Lord knows that," Kish told him.

"I bet it won't be Benjamin," said Jonathan sadly, and then subsided into silence.

The donkeys plodded on. Jonathan stopped feeling luxurious and started to be impatient. If only he could take off this stupid coat and *run* to Mizpah. It was in the territory of Benjamin, their own tribe, but they still weren't there!

They must be getting closer, though: they were seeing more and more people on the road. Some greeted Kish or Abner or Saul like old friends, and smiled at Jonathan or said what a strapping lad he was. Some, Kish steered his donkey deliberately away from. Some were complete strangers, who nodded in polite greeting or just overtook them. Most were on foot, though, and going more slowly than Jonathan and Kish and the others. Jonathan patted his donkey's neck proudly, glad that they'd been found, even if it hadn't been by his father.

When they came over the last ridge and saw the crowds sprawling all around Mizpah's small hill, Kish pulled his donkey out of the road and beckoned to Jonathan to follow.

"Just down here," he said gruffly. "I want you to see something. We can catch the others up."

Curious, Jonathan dug his heels into his own animal and urged it to follow his grandfather. The donkeys stumbled across the uneven hillside, going down diagonally and then up again on the other side of a thicket of thorn trees. Above them the hilltop was jagged, with a single squareish rock sticking up almost vertically like a tooth. Jonathan wondered if that was what Kish wanted to show him: was there a view from up there or something? Maybe you could see all the hills and valleys of Benjamin, and Judah beyond it.

But no: Kish changed course and led him straight along the hillside. Where were they going? To the right, downhill, Mizpah was still in view. Jonathan itched to be down there, among the swirling, chattering crowds.

They came to a stop next to another stone, this one greyish and pointed and very tall—as tall as Saul, Jonathan guessed. It had a few shapes roughly carved into it: letters. The lichen made them hard to read. "Eb-en... e-zer," spelled Jonathan slowly. He looked up at his grandfather. "Stone of help."

"This is why the assembly is at Mizpah, I think," said Kish quietly. He reached down from his donkey to let his large, rough fingers trace the letters.

"Samuel put this stone here as a reminder, after the war with the Philistines. Thus far the Lord has helped us, Samuel said." Kish's face was very serious. "The Lord has helped us. That's what we've got to remember. Always, throughout every generation, God has led the people of Israel. He is our God. He is the one who gave us our land."

He paused, looking at Jonathan expectantly.

"He led our people out of slavery in Egypt," Jonathan said. "And brought them here, to the promised land. He guided them on the way. And when they got here, he—he was their strength…"

"He has fought battles for us, sent prophets to us, helped us in every way," said Kish. "In big things *and* little things, do you understand?" He clapped Jonathan on the back. "You're a young man now, not a boy. That's why I'm showing you this. Remember, all your days: the Lord is our help. Always has been."

As Jonathan nodded, Kish smiled with satisfaction. "And now," he boomed, "the Lord is going to give us a king!"

As they made their way back to the main road, Jonathan found that a new question had formed in his mind, one he'd never thought of before.

If God had led them so well this far, why did they need a king?

But this time he kept his question to himself.

CHAPTER 3

Could It Be Us?

At last, Mizpah. Jonathan tried not to gape as they threaded their way through the throng. He had never seen as many people as this. Not in his whole life put together.

Abner had often described the vast armies who'd gathered to fight the Philistines during the last war. It was the main thing he liked to talk about. There had been thousands upon thousands of warriors. "Shoulder to shoulder," Abner liked to say. "All hurling ourselves forward as one."

Jonathan had watched the scarred face of his father's cousin with awe as he'd described it. He'd closed his eyes and tried to imagine it, all those warriors in one place and that first dash at the enemy. But even the best imagination couldn't have prepared him for the sight of the crowd at Mizpah.

One side of the field was taken up with tents and

baggage and tethered donkeys. Bored servants lounged beside cold cooking fires, or received orders from anxious masters and mistresses. Brightly dressed hawkers gathered their wares and stepped out into the chaotic mass of people to make some sales. Jonathan followed one of them with his eyes, watching him bow and smile at potential customers. The man wove his way around one part of the crowd, then crossed some sort of line into another.

Jonathan squinted and saw a rope pegged into the ground where the man had just been. There were others, too, dividing the crowd into segments. *There must be twelve,* he thought, *one for each tribe.* He watched each one with interest, noticing the differences in their looks or clothing. Where were the seafarers from Zebulun and Asher—were they the ones with short pointed beards, or the ones who all seemed to have at least one piece of clothing that was red? Or were those the desert dwellers from the south?

"There's no room there... Let me find a space for the donkeys," Saul was saying, and Jonathan dropped absent-mindedly to the ground, letting his father take his animal. He was still transfixed by the glorious crowd. There, there was Benjamin, the whole tribe together... He felt a surge of pride.

Abner led the way to the part of the crowd where their relatives were, the other members of the clan of Matri. They nodded at Kish's cousin's family and his sister's nephews and their wives. But there was no time to say anything: already the crowds were beginning to fall silent.

There was a platform at one end of the field, raised high on stilts so that everyone could see. An old man was climbing up some steps at one side. He moved slowly: Jonathan could almost hear the creaking in his bones.

This must be Samuel. The one who heard God's voice! This was the moment. This was the moment when they were going to get their king. A king for all of Israel.

Jonathan swallowed.

The prophet started to speak. His voice was stronger and louder than Jonathan had expected. "This is what the Lord, the God of Israel, says," he began.

Everyone was completely hushed. There wasn't even the sound of breathing.

But Samuel sighed heavily. "He says: I brought Israel up out of Egypt. I delivered you from all the kingdoms that oppressed you. But you have now rejected your God. You have said, No, appoint a king over us."

Jonathan blinked.

Samuel didn't think they should have a king.

God didn't think they should have a king.

Then what was this assembly for?

But Samuel said, "So, now, present yourselves before the Lord by your tribes and clans, and the Lord will choose a king."

Jonathan looked up at his grandfather uncertainly. What was God doing? Was he helping them? Was a king a good thing, or not?

But there was no time to think. Samuel had beckoned a priest up the steps. He was wearing—what was it?—a kind of apron. Jonathan craned to see. It was blue and purple and red, with threads of gold running through it that gleamed in the afternoon sun. Above the waist-band was a sort of breastplate, with jewels arranged in a square on the front.

An ephod! Jonathan realised. This was how the priests found out what God wanted. They plunged their hands into a pocket in the breastplate and brought out two stones, the Urim and the Thummim. The stones had one carved face and one smooth face, and God would make it so that one came out face-up and one face-down. Usually, if Urim was face-up it meant yes and if Thummim was face-up it meant no. Jonathan could hardly believe he was actually going to *see* them.

The priest was intoning some sort of prayer. He washed his hands in a bronze basin. Then he looked at Samuel, waiting for instructions.

Samuel beckoned the first tribe forward. Judah. They surged into the open space in front of the platform, hundreds of them, all talking excitedly to each other. Jonathan saw a particularly strong-looking man run his fingers through his oiled hair. He had a gold collar around his neck and his bare arms were muscly. Even from here you could see that his face was twisted with a mixture of pride and hope.

He thinks it'll be him, Jonathan thought. He watched the man shove a grey-haired woman out of the way so that he could get to the front. Jonathan shuddered. *Please let it not be him.*

Samuel said something, and the priest thrust his hands into the pocket of the ephod. He held out the stones for the prophet to see. Samuel shook his head.

"Not Judah," he shouted. There was a roar of disappointment from the Judahites, but they trailed back to their places obediently. The muscly man hung his head. The rest of the crowd stirred and rustled.

The tribe of Reuben came up next. But it wasn't them either. It wasn't Simeon, or Issachar.

It wasn't Zebulun or Dan or Naphtali.

Soon there were only three tribes left. Benjamin, Ephraim, and Manasseh. The Benjaminites came forwards quietly; their crowd was the smallest by far. Jonathan wondered if everyone else's heart was fluttering as much as his was.

The priest was washing his hands again, and Samuel was saying a prayer. The priest put his hand in the ephod... he brought out the stones.

Samuel looked at them carefully. He looked up. He shouted, "It is Benjamin! Now you will present yourselves by your clans."

It was Benjamin! *It was Benjamin!* The king was going

to come from their tribe! Jonathan had forgotten all his doubts and questions. His heart swelled with joy as the crowd around him boomed with soft murmurs.

The Benjaminites returned to their roped-off section of the crowd, then came forward again clan by clan. The clan of Matri came third. As Jonathan walked forward, the people around him shivered and looked at each other. *What if it's us?* they were thinking. *Could it be us?*

The Urim and Thummim came out of their pouch. Samuel nodded. "It is the clan of Matri."

Jonathan's heart thumped.

Next it was families. The house of Kish was chosen. Jonathan felt sick and elated and important and tiny all at once. Who was it going to be? Kish himself? Abner? Maybe, just maybe—Jonathan allowed himself to think it—maybe it would be him, Jonathan, the first king of Israel…

If it's me, he vowed silently, *I'll always remember. The Lord is the one who helps us. We're his people. He's our God.*

This time Samuel wrote all their names on stones with a stick of charcoal and tumbled them into a clay jar. He put his own hand in. He pulled out a stone.

The crowd was perfectly silent.

"SAUL!" cried Samuel, and Jonathan thought he might die, his heart was beating so wildly in his chest. His father—his father, the king—his *father*—

But Kish's urgent voice growled, "Where is he? Where

is he?" and Jonathan realised with a shudder that Saul was not there.

He was not in the crowd at all.

CHAPTER 4

Long Live the King

Saul crouched by the donkeys. They smelled, but not badly. He'd pulled the bags off their backs and tied them up carefully—then stayed there. He couldn't join the crowd, he just couldn't.

He heard Samuel's voice calling out—the crowd roared suddenly—Saul squeezed his eyes shut. Was there no way of stopping this from happening?

Two months ago, when he'd first met Samuel on his search for the donkeys, and Samuel had told him he was going to be the king, it had seemed like a wonderful thing. The prophet had taken a flask of oil and anointed him with it, pouring it over Saul's head like a blessing. He had kissed him as if he were his own son. Samuel's voice hadn't been loud and commanding then as it was now: it had been soft and full of emotion. "Has not the Lord anointed you ruler over his inheritance?" he'd said.

Saul shuddered as he remembered it. He had only gone to Samuel to see if he knew where his father's donkeys were. He hadn't asked for this! But Samuel had said so many things, and it really had seemed wonderful at the time… He'd told Saul that the Spirit of God would come upon him—upon *him*, Saul!—and would change him. He'd told him that God was with him.

After that, for a while, Saul had felt a strange certainty. He *did* feel different: braver and more solid somehow. He had prayed like he'd never prayed before, feeling sure that God was really listening. He'd sung and danced in worship. He'd travelled back to Gibeah full of joy.

But he'd kept it a secret. How could you tell your family that a prophet had anointed you as king? And then gradually the sense of excitement and solidness had crumbled. He was just Saul. Tall, yes, strong, yes, and from a good family… but not a king. Not the ruler of all Israel.

And yet here he was. He could hear other sounds from the crowd now: it wasn't unified like it had been before. There were individual shouts. Were they angry, or excited? And was that… was that his name they were shouting? Maybe he'd just imagined it. Saul pulled his long cloak around himself miserably. *Please, please,* he thought, *let it all have been a mistake. Even prophets must make mistakes sometimes.*

But the queasy feeling in the bottom of his stomach told him they did not.

What *was* going on? Suddenly Saul wished he hadn't decided to hide. It was horrible not knowing what was going on in the crowd. He should be with his father, his son…

He imagined Jonathan's eyes shining with pride as he learned that his own father would be king.

He stood up suddenly, making the donkeys flick their ears in surprise. Maybe being king could be a good thing. Samuel would be by his side telling him what God wanted him to do, and there would almost certainly be people who could take a lead when it came to battles… And people would look up to him, not just with their eyes like they did anyway because he was tall, but really look up to him. They'd try to please him. They'd want to know what he thought about things.

He shuddered. What *did* he think about things? What if he got it wrong? What if Samuel was away one day and he had to make a decision on his own? What about when Samuel *died*? Saul crouched down again, burying his face in the pile of baggage.

"Saul! Saul!" He could hear the shouts more clearly now. They were coming this way. He couldn't escape.

Please… he thought, but he barely knew who he was asking for help, or what help he wanted.

Samuel had said, "Has not the Lord anointed you ruler over his inheritance?" But that was the *point*, they were God's people, it was God's land, it was God's inheritance he was going to have to be king of, and nobody could ever do things as well as God did. Saul wasn't going to get it right. He wasn't one of the great heroes of the past. He was… he was only little. Even if he *was* tall.

The voices had come even closer. Saul peeked over the donkey's side, and his heart sank. It was Kish and a few younger men from their clan. They were looking around intently. "Saul? Saul!" they cried.

Saul squeezed his eyes shut for a moment. Then he sprang up. "At last," he said, trying to sound casual, "donkeys sorted! Oh, hello, were you looking for me? Is Samuel ready?"

Kish raised an eyebrow, as if to say, *You're fooling no one, son.* But the other men shouted at him in excitement.

"It's you!" they said. "Samuel has taken the lots already, you missed it! It's you, you're the king!"

Saul tried to look thunderstruck. "M—me?" he gasped. "The king of Israel? Why—but—"

He let himself be dragged forwards by their eager hands. They wanted him to run, but he walked, trying to be dignified. His cloak swept around him and he held his head high. Glancing at Kish's face, he saw that his father looked grudgingly impressed.

Saul was a head taller than these other men. As they made their way through the crowd towards the platform where Samuel waited, a few people gave little gasps of admiration. Others muttered with what sounded like doubt. Saul squared his jaw and tried to look heroic.

At the front of the crowd Samuel's gaze met Saul like a

flame. Saul swallowed, afraid—but the prophet took his hand and raised it in the air.

"Do you see the man the Lord has chosen?" he cried. "There's no one like him among all the people!"

Saul looked at the crowd. The crowd looked at Saul.

Then they roared, "Long live the king!"

After that Samuel talked at length about what a king should do and how the people should treat him, and people from every tribe brought Saul gifts: fabric and wine and jewels and costly incense, fat sheep and cakes of raisins and jars of olive oil. It was a good thing Kish had insisted on bringing so many servants: there was a lot to carry.

Saul stood by trying to look kingly while Kish gave orders to sort and arrange all the gifts, and they were just about to set off home again when three men dashed forwards and threw themselves down in front of Saul's feet. They laid their swords on the ground. Proper swords: they had notches and marks on them. They must have seen a lot of battles.

"We will follow you," one of the men said. "The king our God has appointed."

Saul recognised the expression in their faces. His son Jonathan had looked at him like that when he was very small—his eyes brimming with admiration and loyalty. Michal, who was smaller, still did look at him like that.

But these were grown men, proper warriors with big hands and sinewy arms. And they wanted to follow him.

Oh Lord, help, said Saul inwardly. But he kept his face still and bowed his head. "I'll be glad to have you as my followers," he said.

They left Mizpah in a little procession: Kish grunted that Saul should ride at the front. He sat stiffly and silently, and barely noticed the little crowd they passed, struggling up the hillside on foot.

But Jonathan did. One of them, a ragged woman with no shoes, spat on the ground as Saul went past. "How can *he* save us?" she muttered.

Jonathan snapped his gaze away quickly so she wouldn't see that he'd heard. He looked ahead at the straight, silent back of his father. He bit his lip.

The people had asked for a king, and God had given them one. Jonathan supposed that that would be all right as long as everyone remembered that their real king was God himself. He was their helper. Maybe God wanted the king to help everyone remember that.

But if that was true… if the king was supposed to be a good leader and help people love God, then… then…

Jonathan knew it was disloyal, but he couldn't help thinking it.

Why had God chosen *Saul*?

CHAPTER 5

A Strange Horse

On the hillside, by the pomegranate tree, the breeze made Michal's dark clothes flap and billow. She liked the feel of it and twisted her body up and round, inviting the wind to wrap itself over her, and shivering a bit as it did. She liked coming up here, in between chores: she could see the whole farm, and Gibeah as well, and watch people coming and going.

She felt the wind change direction: it was coming up from the farm now. It carried noises with it: the murmur of the serving-women, and the braying of the donkeys, and…

And… wailing?

Michal squinted downhill. Someone new had come to the farmhouse: there was a horse standing outside. And from inside she could clearly, definitely hear the sound of wailing.

Someone was upset—very upset. Several people, actually, by the sound of it.

Eyes narrowing, Michal started down the hill.

Should she go to the big field and get her father? No, she decided. He might be cross if it turned out to be nothing. He was in the middle of ploughing and he liked to be alone. She'd better go straight down to the house without him.

Saul seemed to want to be alone as much as possible now that he was the king. Michal couldn't understand it. Before, he used to swing her in his arms sometimes or take her on his knee and tell her stories about how their ancestors had left Egypt and come to their own land, or about the heroes of the tribe of Benjamin, or about how God made the world... But ever since they'd come back from Mizpah he had just shaken her off when she tried to hug him, or said, "Not now, Michal."

Maybe it was because he was too important now, she'd told herself sadly every day as she'd trailed out to bring him his noon meal and he had brushed her off yet again. Now he was king, he had to lead battles and things.

"But he *isn't* leading any battles," she muttered crossly for the hundredth time as she skirted the edge of the smaller field and stepped over the empty streambed at the bottom. He wasn't doing anything king-ish at all. He was just *ploughing*.

Ahead of her, the strange horse outside the house was pawing the ground. She'd never seen such a big horse: it was almost as big as an ox. She saw Jonathan run up to the house behind it, his bow in his hand. She called out to him but he didn't hear—he just flew straight inside.

Michal started running too, not wanting him to find out what was happening before she did. The wailing was getting louder and louder, and she shivered with fear and anticipation. Where had the horse come from? It must be a messenger's horse. So what was the news?

Maybe they'd changed their minds about Saul being king, she thought suddenly. Jonathan had told her that Saul still had to be anointed properly, in front of everyone. Samuel was going to pour oil on his head and he'd get a proper crown. Until that had happened he wasn't really king.

Maybe *that* was why he hadn't done anything king-ish yet.

Jonathan had said that the king was supposed to help people. He'd persuaded Saul to take some shepherd friend of his away from his master and employ him on their own farm instead. Oren, his name was. That was a king-ish thing to do, Jonathan had said. But Michal didn't see how. It was supposed to be about battles and things, and leading people, wasn't it?

So maybe the messenger was coming to say that Saul hadn't been a good enough king and everyone had changed their minds.

Or… or maybe the messenger was coming to give him his first king-ish thing to do.

Her heart beat even faster at that thought. She was

here now; the door was wedged open with the usual stone. Michal ran straight inside, not even stopping to pat the huge horse on the cheek.

Then she slowed down, feeling scared suddenly. She could make out the voices of individual wailers now: her mother, and one of the serving women, and her sister Merab. Beneath the shrill sobs she heard her grandfather's gruff voice saying something, and another voice replying—a man's voice, a stranger.

She slid into the room and pushed herself against the wall. "What's happened?" she whispered.

But nobody answered her.

Saul undid the straps that held the heavy iron plough to the cows' yoke, heaving it aside and patting their steaming flanks to say well done. The last furrow had been laid in the earth, and the field was brown and ready for sowing. Saul shook out his aching arms, feeling proud of a job completed.

He left the plough where it was and drove the oxen back towards the house, where fresh fodder awaited them. Him, too, he hoped... Eggs, and fresh bread, and perhaps a little honey to brighten his eyes.

Michal hadn't brought him out his food today, which was odd. But that was all right, he thought generously: he'd smell the sweet smoke of the cooking fire soon, and he'd eat his fill, and then perhaps in the afternoon he'd take Jonathan hunting. He'd been neglecting that boy.

But as he neared the house there was no cooking smell. And there were hoofprints in the ground. Big ones.

Saul was suddenly filled with a sense of foreboding. Who had been here? Who had travelled so far and so fast that they needed a *horse*? Biting his lip, he left the oxen where they were and went hesitantly into the house.

They all stared at him as he came in, like they'd been waiting for his arrival. Kish with a face of thunder, the children in tears. Jonathan looked old with sorrow. The three warriors from Mizpah were there, and Abner, all of them with dark eyes and grimly downturned lips.

Saul swallowed. "What's wrong?"

"A messenger came," Kish answered heavily. "From Jabesh Gilead, up north by the river. The Ammonites have attacked. They've attacked Israel."

Saul sat down, staying calm, rubbing his left foot where it had got sweaty inside his leather sandal. "How bad is it?"

"The Ammonites are around the city. No one can get out or in. They say they'll make peace only once they have gouged out the right eye of every man, woman and child."

"Gouged out their eyes!" Saul stopped rubbing his foot.

In a high voice, Jonathan said, "They want to bring disgrace on Israel."

"The Ammonites let them send messengers out to beg the rest of Israel for help," said Kish. "It's clear enough they don't think anyone will come."

Saul stood up again. He felt a kind of roaring in his chest. He recognised the feeling: it was as if he'd been hollow and now he had been filled up. It was like how he'd felt after he'd met Samuel. But that time it had been love and wonder that had filled him. Now it was rage and indignation and a burning for justice. He felt like he was being taken over by something.

Taken over by God, he realised dimly.

"How dare they?" he heard his own voice say. "How dare they!"

There was a knife lying by the fire, the old blackened one the serving women used for chopping up meat as it went into the pan. He snatched it up. Without another word he stormed outside. He knew what he had to do. The oxen did not have time to pull away in fear before he'd slit their throats and their bulky bodies lay bleeding on the ground.

He made short work of them, chopping them each into six huge pieces, leaving the rough hide on. Everyone had come to watch by this point, wondering what he would do next, not daring to interrupt. He beckoned to his cousin and the three warriors from Mizpah, pointing them each to three great chunks of meat.

"Take them to all the tribes," he said, breathing heavily. "Tell them, this is what will be done to the oxen of everyone who does not follow Saul and Samuel. Tell them we will muster at—at—"

"At Bezek," said Abner, his eyes glinting. "That's the best place."

"Tell them we will muster at Bezek," said Saul. "In two days' time." He gazed around at them, taking in their wide eyes, their shining faces. "We will destroy these Ammonites." He shook his bloody fist. "We will rescue Jabesh Gilead!"

CHAPTER 6

Charge!

It worked. Two days later Saul found himself standing on the hillside at Bezek, surveying the army. They'd come from every tribe and there were thousands of them—*thousands*. Three hundred and thirty captains had reported to him, and each one brought a huge band of men.

Abner stood beside him, nodding his approval. "The Lord is with you, it seems."

"He will not let disgrace come to Israel," answered Saul quietly. He thought of the people of Jabesh Gilead—of the messengers he'd met earlier that day, with their fearful faces and their intact eyes… He gritted his teeth in a wordless prayer.

"Were the messages sent?" he asked his cousin. "The people of Jabesh know we're coming?"

"They have told the enemy they will surrender tomorrow," confirmed Abner.

"And the men have their orders?"

"Yes."

Saul nodded.

It was working. The Lord was with him! Him, Saul! For so many months—for so many *years,* really—he'd been pretending that he was more confident than he was. Putting on a smile when he was shaking inside. But now something was different... He *was* more confident. The Spirit of the Lord was in him and he knew what he was doing.

It was amazing.

He ordered the army not to light any fires overnight. There must be no chance of the enemy realising they were there. Then he sat down by his tent and waited. There were men huddled together all around him, but Saul heard no talking. There was only the rasp of whetstones sharpening spears, and the squeak of cloths polishing whatever scraps of armour they'd managed to find.

They waited, and they waited. The moon made its way across the sky. Somewhere on the plain, jackals howled and an owl hooted, sending shivers down Saul's spine. Jabesh Gilead was just across there—so close— they could see the flicker of the Ammonites' watch-fires all around it. And still they waited.

It was long after midnight when Saul gave the order. He sent the left and right flank out first, creeping round in the dark to attack from north and south. The central division he led himself, straight across the plain.

Saul had been in battles before, but they'd been minor skirmishes compared to this. He held his spear steady in one sweating hand, squeezing the strap of his cowhide shield with the other. He was taller than any of the other men, and he could feel their gaze on his back. He tried to hold his head high. *The Lord chose me,* he reminded himself. *The Lord is with me.*

They were there. The Ammonite camp was soundless, slumbering. Now was the crucial moment—Saul could see the white eyes of the Ammonite sentry widen suddenly—

An arrow shot the man down, but not before he had given a yell of alarm. Someone within the camp took up the shout. The Ammonites were waking. The time was now! Without hesitating Saul hefted his spear, raised his shield in the air, and screamed at the top of his lungs.

"ISRAAAAEEEL! Israel and the Lord God!"

Then they charged.

They fought for hours. The Ammonites had been caught by surprise, but they were well-trained men, and well-armed. The initial rush of Saul's three divisions sent the enemy scattering, staggering from their beds and running for their lives—but they soon regrouped. It was an ugly battle, fought hand-to-hand over collapsed tents and burnt-out cooking fires.

But they won.

The sun was high in the sky, and Saul walked back towards Bezek in a daze. His body stank with dried sweat and his ears still rang with the shouts and gasps of dying men. Around him the other exhausted Israelites were straggling back to camp: Saul could see grim triumph on all their faces. They'd feast tonight.

Someone clapped him on the back. "No need to look long-faced! We did it!"

The man obviously didn't know who he was. "We did it," Saul agreed, smiling effortfully. "No more Ammonites. No eye-gouging."

He walked back together with his new friend, swapping stories from the battlefield and telling each other what they were looking forward to when they got home. Saul said a nod from his father, a kiss from his daughters, and the admiration of his oldest son. He didn't speak of kingship.

As they reached Bezek they saw a white-haired figure standing outside the camp.

"The prophet!" said Saul's new friend in hushed tones. "Look! They say he hears from God himself. He doesn't need an ephod like the other priests."

Saul glanced around rapidly—but Samuel couldn't be avoided. He was coming forward to meet them. Soon he was clasping Saul's arms and nodding his approval.

"Wait—" whispered Saul's companion— "wait, you're… You're Saul! The king!" Going white, he sank to the ground, bowing low. "Sir… If I'd known…"

Saul touched him awkwardly on the shoulder. "It's all right," he said. "Get up."

Samuel was about to say something, but the man interrupted, springing up and speaking as fast as he could. "Sir," he gabbled, speaking to the old prophet now. "Samuel, sir, there were some who scoffed at Saul reigning over us. I know men myself who did." He glanced at Saul rapidly, then back to Samuel. "Traitors! Let's put them to death."

Saul swallowed. He'd *known* people didn't want him to be king... They'd kept it quiet, of course, but he'd been sure of it. People didn't think he would be any good.

"The Lord made you king, sir," said the man. "How dare anyone disbelieve it?"

He was looking at Saul with a hungry expression on his face. Samuel was looking at him too. Other men stood by, watching from a distance.

He could have them killed, all the people who'd said he'd be no good. He could do it. He'd won the battle; he'd saved Jabesh Gilead; everyone would be on his side now. They'd do what he said. They'd execute anyone he asked them to.

No. No. Saul shook his head. "No man shall be put to death today," he said. "Today is for feasting. Today, the Lord has rescued Israel."

He saw Samuel's solemn white beard twitch into a smile.

"Today we feast," the old man agreed. "And tomorrow,

we will send out messengers with the good news." His gaze was steady and approving: it was the kind of look Saul had always hoped his father would give him, or his son. "We will gather all Israel again, and I will anoint you before their eyes." Samuel bowed his pale head. "The Lord has already made you his king. But now, I think, all the people will recognise it."

PART TWO

The Son of the King

Three Years Later

CHAPTER 7

A Far Bigger Army

Jonathan was taller now: as tall as his father, but more lightly built. He trod the ground more gently than Saul and he ran faster. His arms bent his grandfather's bow with ease, and people said he was the best shot in Israel. His step was sure as he made his way through the camp.

But his heart fluttered, at least a little. This was his first camp, his first proper army gathering. The Philistines had invaded Israelite land, and the people had gathered to drive them out. Here they were, thousands of men. They'd brought with them anything they could find that had a sharp edge: sickles, mattocks, even heavy iron ploughs. Jonathan was glad of his bow, and his light, strong sword. There were advantages to being the king's son.

"Jonathan! Jonathan!" someone called after him from the side of a fire. "Is it true it was you? You were at Geba?"

"Yes," Jonathan answered, slowing to clasp the man's hand as he passed.

He was uneasy, despite his smile. At the time it had seemed the right thing to do. The Philistines had no right to be in Geba, in the heart of Benjamin. It was Israelite land. It was God's land. Jonathan had been desperate to drive them out—so desperate, he'd taken things into his own hands. He'd led some of the men out of Gibeah, scrambled the short distance north and taken the enemy by surprise.

And he'd defeated them. His first battle, and he'd won.

Except that more Philistines had then come to take the old ones' place. And more, and more. Now it wasn't just a battle: they were facing a full-on war.

The Philistines were close to Gibeah, but Saul had summoned the army to gather here, at Gilgal, to the east. And here they were still: far away from the hills where the Philistines were, far away from their own homes, and *not fighting*. And Jonathan dreaded to think just how many enemy fighters must be waiting near Gibeah by now.

"You're the reason we're here," said the man by the fire. Jonathan couldn't tell whether it was an accusation or an expression of thanks.

"I suppose I am," he answered lightly, and moved on.

He made for the edge of the camp. "Where are the new arrivals?" he asked someone. "Any word of Samuel?"

"That way," said the man, shaking his head.

Jonathan hurried onwards without waiting to hear what the headshake meant.

Samuel had said he'd take no longer than seven days to join them. They weren't to go back up to attack the Philistines without having first made sacrifices to God—seeking his help, seeking his guidance. The old prophet was the one who had to do it.

So they'd waited, and more and more fighters had come to join them, and it looked like it was going to be all right… and then the news of the Philistines' far bigger army had started to reach them, and the Israelites had started to tremble.

Now it was almost the end of the fifth day, and there was no Samuel.

"Welcome." At the edge of the camp, Jonathan greeted the new arrivals as if he'd been expecting them. But his heart sank as he took them in: an old man, four women, and a gaggle of exhausted-looking children. There were two men of fighting age as well, but they looked scrawny, hungry.

These weren't fighters. They were refugees.

How had things got this bad this quickly?

"Will we be safe?" one of the children asked him. "Are we safe now?"

Jonathan knelt down and looked into the little girl's eyes. "I am Jonathan, son of Saul," he told her gently. "I will do my best to keep you safe." Then he straightened up. "Where have you come from?"

"The hill country," answered the old man. "Between Gibeah and Michmash."

Michmash! "We've heard the Philistines are mustering there," Jonathan said.

"Thousands and thousands of them," confirmed the old man. "With horses and chariots and everything, not like our rabble." His voice was bitter. "Everyone's running away. And everyone who can't run is hiding."

Jonathan nodded. He'd heard about it already. Every dank cave and rocky hole in Benjamin was being used as a hiding place. Even the wells and water cisterns. Even the tombs.

Benjamin was in trouble. *Israel* was in trouble.

And with news like that, how long could they keep the army hopeful?

"And Samuel. Have you any word of him?" asked Jonathan, trying to hide the anxiety in his voice.

The old man shook his head.

"Thank you," Jonathan said with a polite bow that he hoped would disguise his sinking feeling. "Come this way... There's food for you, and a friendly fire... Yes, this way."

He scooped up the littlest child and carried her along. "Samuel will be all right," he said reassuringly, though he was speaking more to himself than to her. "The Lord God knows what's best. If we have to wait, we have to wait."

The sixth day came. Then the seventh. Still no Samuel.

Jonathan ducked under the flap of his father's tent and stepped inside, standing to attention. He was late: he'd been with the elders of the town, begging them for more provision for those fleeing the hill country. There were more of them every day. The army camp was no place for them, and Gilgal itself was filling up quickly.

"Send them on," one of the elders had shrugged helplessly. "Send them over the river. We can do nothing for them here."

Jonathan's heart was heavy. *If only you'd left the Philistines at Geba well alone,* he told himself. *Then we wouldn't be in this mess.*

But they were *Philistines*, another part of him still insisted. In God's land. They were a stain on Israel.

And what good will it do Israel if the Philistines wipe us out? said the first part of him.

Jonathan closed his eyes for a moment, trying to ignore his own thoughts. He had to listen to his father and the other commanders, gathered around the table in the middle of the tent. This was a council of war.

"The men are scattering," Abner was saying tersely. "We need to move."

"We can't," answered Saul. "We can't without Samuel."

Jonathan nodded eagerly, focusing at last. "He'll be here," he said. "The seventh day is not ended yet."

"Yes," said Saul, "we must wait." But his voice came out in a whine.

"You're the king," growled Abner. "God chose you. You're in charge."

"Yes…" said Saul, wavering.

Jonathan shook his head. "Samuel told us to wait. That means God told us to wait."

But Abner disagreed. "If we attack now," he said flatly, "we'll be fighting in our own territory. We know those valleys and hills. We stand a chance of victory. But if we wait, they'll come down to meet us on the plain. Which is the kind of land those chariots of theirs are specifically designed for." He leaned forwards, slamming his hands on the table suddenly. "They'll wipe us out."

Saul looked around. His eyes were wide, desperate.

"Samuel might never come," added Abner. "He might be dead for all we know."

Jonathan watched his father's face. *Please,* he thought, *please…*

Saul opened his mouth. What was he going to say? *Come on,* thought Jonathan, *tell him you're going to wait, that's the right thing to do…*

"Bring the offerings," said Saul finally, nodding to the priest. "I will make the sacrifices and ask for God's help."

Jonathan gaped. "But—no—"

"Jonathan," said Saul—his voice was crisp and clear now— "you will not interfere. Do as I say."

Jonathan curled his hands into fists. "But *you're* supposed to do what *God* says." He glared at his father—

glared so strongly that he half expected his eyes to burn a hole in him. He wished they could.

"Do you really think," he cried, "that we're supposed to just make our own plans and then ask God to smile on them? No! We're supposed to do what God says! He's not like a—a hired warrior! You don't just pay him to do what you want! He's the one the plans are supposed to come *from*."

"I am the king," answered Saul. "God chose me."

"But—"

"Bring the offerings," Saul repeated coldly. "No more waiting. I will make the sacrifices, and we will pray for God's help. Then we will fight."

CHAPTER 8

A Foolish Thing

They didn't wait to gather the troops to witness the sacrifices. Saul told the priest it was because they were in a hurry, but he had another secret reason of his own: the grisly feeling deep in the pit of his stomach. Was it shame? He felt Jonathan's gaze on him, and avoided meeting his eye.

But he was the *king*, and it was his job to lead the people, and it was possible the Philistines were marching from Michmash even as they spoke.

The animals for the sacrifice were brought in. The priest nodded: these would do. Outside the tent, men were building the altar, laying the wood already on a closely packed square of stones. Saul strode out to see, clapping his sweaty hands together and forcing himself to speak cheerfully: "That's it. I've never seen an altar built so fast. The Lord will be pleased with this offering, I'm sure."

Abner came to stand by his side, his arms crossed triumphantly over his broad chest. Jonathan came out too, but his eyes were fixed on the ground. Saul felt a pang of anger at his son's lack of respect. Arrogance, that was what it was! He'd think of a way to punish him later.

The bull's feet had been tied; the priest's hand rested briefly on its head. Then his knife fell. Soon they were watching the flames roar high above the piled meat on the altar. Saul stared fixedly into the fire, not speaking, until the flames began to settle into a steady sputter.

"Whatever wrong we have done," prayed the priest, "forgive us. Look kindly on us, O Lord."

Saul bowed his head, trying to look devoted.

Then a new voice cut harshly into his ears. A familiar voice. A voice filled with fury.

"What have you done?"

Samuel was striding towards them, moving with a strength that should have been beyond his years. His thin white hair blew back behind him. His wrinkled face was contorted with anger and shock.

Saul's heart jangled in his chest. He stuttered, "The men were scattering… You did not come…"

Samuel came to a stop beside the fire. The bright flames cast a shadow over one side of his face. He looked Saul dead in the eye. "You have done a *foolish* thing," he cried, breathing heavily. "You have not kept the command the Lord your God gave you."

Saul felt unbearably hot all of a sudden. He said

nothing. He had no argument to make.

"If you had obeyed," Samuel went on, "he would have established your kingdom over Israel for all time. But now... now your kingdom will not last. The Lord has sought out a man after his own heart, and appointed *him* ruler of the people, because you have not kept the Lord's command."

The prophet's voice was laden with disdain. A new king... Saul half expected Samuel to produce this man straight away, to pour the oil over his forehead, to summon all the people to acclaim him king. Saul would be swept away, banished from the land of Israel, banished from the land of the Lord...

But no: the prophet had nothing more to say, it seemed. For now, at least. He was already walking away.

Squeezing his eyes tightly shut for a moment, Saul couldn't help picturing him, this man after God's own heart. He'd be strong, wise, good-looking too probably. He'd take the Philistines by storm... the kingdom would be at peace for ever...

He snapped his eyes open to see Jonathan's white face, staring at him across the fire. Everyone else was avoiding his gaze.

"You're still king for now, Saul," said Abner softly.

"Make the other offering," Saul muttered, turning away. "I'm going to take some rest."

Two days later in Gibeah, Michal was surrounded by sheep. Smelly, dirty creatures. They didn't like her, and they let her know it. One butted her on the bottom; another bellowed in her face. And now half the flock was heading off in the wrong direction…

"Come back!" she cried helplessly. "Look, I'm sorry, I know I'm not your usual shepherd."

Or any kind of shepherd, she thought grumpily as she sprinted ahead of them. This had always been her brothers' job, and Jonathan's friend Oren's, but they had all gone off to Gilgal. Michal had never been taught to herd sheep. She was learning fast.

"Aha!" she grunted, managing to overtake the rebels and shove her knees into their obstinate flanks. "*That* way. Go."

They bleated at her, but did as they were told. They did know where home was, after all. At last, at last, she got them into the sheepfold, closed the gate, and sank to the ground, panting.

"A big task for a little one," said a voice.

Michal sprang to her feet again. "Jonathan!" It was him: tall and bronze-skinned, a red cloak tossed over his shoulder, a sword hanging in its battered case by his side. He'd come back! The army must be ready to fight at last! Michal flung herself at her brother and squeezed him tight. "I'm not so little," she said.

"No," he answered seriously, hugging her back. "I'm sorry you've been left to cope by yourself, though. I thought you'd be safe. Where are the men we left to protect the farm?"

Michal had kept the fears of the past week closely contained, dammed up in a dark lake inside her where she didn't have to think about them. Now suddenly she felt them threaten to overflow.

"They left," she whispered. "They were afraid of the Philistines."

He looked troubled, and she felt bad for saying it; but then he laughed. "It's Abner I'd be afraid of, if I were them. He's not a man who suffers fools."

"Is he here? Are you all back? Have you fought the Philistines?"

"Not yet."

"What's happened, then?"

He didn't answer her question. "We'll stay here for now."

"What's happened, Jonathan?"

He took her hand and mumbled, "I'm just glad you're safe."

There was obviously no point in asking any more questions, Michal realised. So she followed her brother along the hillside, back to the house. She was right: there were soldiers scattered across the farm, fiddling with the ropes and goatskins they would turn into tents. They were spreading down towards the main town, too.

But there didn't seem to be enough of them.

"Where are the rest?" asked Michal, frowning. "Did you divide the army?"

"No," answered Jonathan. As she turned to face him again she saw that he was trying not to let his face crumple. "This is everyone."

"The entire army? Just these men? But Jonathan…"

"Six hundred soldiers," he told her flatly. "Give or take. The rest have deserted us."

Michal's eyes widened.

Six hundred! And she'd heard that in Michmash the Philistines had thousands. Six hundred…. There was no way the Israelites could win a battle with so few soldiers.

"We'll stay here for now," Jonathan repeated in a tired voice. "We can hold Gibeah, at least."

CHAPTER 9

Michmash

Saul had been sitting under the pomegranate tree on the hillside near Gibeah for what seemed like his whole lifetime. The weeks since he'd brought his six hundred fighters here to face the Philistines had trickled by with no battles. How could they face the enemy with so few men? But what else could Saul do? Nothing but sit there with his face barely moving, not making decisions.

And every time another messenger came, Saul heard Samuel's words echoing in his head. *Your kingdom will not last... You have not kept the Lord's command.*

"The Philistines are getting ready for battle," one messenger said breathlessly. "Our spies have seen them."

Your kingdom will not last, said the voice in Saul's head.

A week later: "The men are as ready as they can be, sir, but we're still too few... We've got no blacksmiths to make more weapons…"

Saul turned away. *Your kingdom will not last…*

"Sir," came another message, "they've sent out more raiders. To the east this time. They're everywhere." *Your kingdom will not last…*

"AAAARGGHH!" It was too much. Saul screamed in rage and despair, slamming his fists against his head as if he could beat out his own brains and those terrible words that filled them.

"Sir…" said the messenger hesitantly, backing away.

"Why will they not attack us? What are they waiting for?" Saul hissed, standing up to loom over him. *When is this going to end?* he added silently. Was God going to take away his kingdom town by town, month by agonising month?

The messenger quailed. "Sir… I…"

"Get out of my sight."

As the young man scrambled away, Saul threw himself back onto his chair. He gripped its carved armrests. Even this disgusted him…. it had been a gift for a king.

Some king.

He was about to toss it away and find another, plainer seat—but suddenly he found himself gripping onto it even harder. "AAARGH!" he yelled for the second time that morning. His feet leaped up off the ground—it was an earthquake—the earth was shaking! He crouched on the chair, but that wasn't stable either.

He fell sideways with a bang, and curled up in fright, clutching at his own knees. There was an awful growling roar in the depths of the earth—he was going to be swallowed up—

Then it stopped.

Saul trembled.

An earthquake—it could only be a sign from God. It could only be a sign of anger against him, Saul.

Yes, he'd failed. He'd failed. He squeezed his eyes tight in despair.

At last, after what felt like a long time, he stood up heavily and dusted himself down. The shock had ebbed away and left bitterness in his mouth. *Haven't you shown enough anger already, God?* he thought. *Didn't you say you were going to take my kingdom away? Is it not bad enough to take it away by giving it to the Philistines, of all people?*

Where was God's great love for Israel, the people he'd chosen for himself and settled in this land? And where was this man after God's own heart who was going to establish the kingdom the way God wanted it? Saul felt his eyes prickle with desperation. Couldn't *he* come and lead the army, whoever he was?

Saul heard footsteps. He scrambled onto his chair again, trying to look composed. "I told you to go," he began to cry—

But this wasn't a soldier.

It was Michal.

"Something's happened," she said. "Something's happened to the Philistines!"

Jonathan had woken early that morning. For a moment
after his eyes opened he lay there on his low pallet
bed, listening to the flap of the stitched goatskins that
formed his shelter. He felt tense, alert. He jumped up
and dressed quietly, not meaning to disturb anyone; but
then he saw a pair of eyes gleam at him in the darkness.
Oren was awake too.

Jonathan whispered to him, "Come on."

Soon they were moving through the cold dark, clutching their weapons in their hands to keep them from
rattling. Oren carried Jonathan's spare spears normally,
but now he had only his own long knife. A cooking
knife really, but he swore by it, and anyway there weren't
enough proper weapons anywhere anymore.

"We'll just go and look," Jonathan said quietly as they
stole out of the camp. "I want to see the Philistines for
myself. We'll go up to Geba and have a look."

The route was familiar to them both; there was no need
to speak. They climbed and crawled and crept over the
dry land, feeling every rock and scrubby plant beneath
their thin sandals. Jonathan had rarely felt so alert.

As they reached Geba the sun was rising, but
they went even more carefully than they had in the
pitch dark. To their left was the pass; here the valley

deepened to a rocky gorge that cut through the hills and wiggled away east towards the wilderness. Jonathan crouched at its edge, Oren by his side, peering down into its pit of darkness. Then across: across to where the Philistines were.

There was an outpost, right there on the other side of the gorge. Just five or six tents, a sheaf of spears stuck in the ground outside each one. Jonathan shivered. Further ahead there'd be more of them, more camps, more soldiers... but these ones were right there. The gorge was narrow. They were almost within touching distance.

He looked at Oren, and saw his own feelings mirrored in his friend's glittering eyes: excitement, fear, uncertainty. Should they do it? Should they go across?

Jonathan looked across the gorge again. Philistines: worshippers of a false god. They shouldn't be here; they should be in their own territory; they were polluting the land the Lord had given to his people. Israel was supposed to be a kingdom of justice, of peace; a people who obeyed the God who ruled over them. *A nation after God's own heart,* Jonathan phrased it in his own mind. They couldn't be that while the Philistines were here.

To attack would be madness. There were only two of them. And yet...

Feeling certainty harden within him, Jonathan looked back at Oren. "Come on," he said again, jerking his head towards the Philistine camp. "Perhaps the Lord will act on our behalf. Nothing can stop him."

Oren reached out to form their two hands into a single clenched fist. "I'm with you," he said. "Heart and soul."

The early sunlight was streaking into the gorge now. If they scrambled down to the bottom they'd be easily visible. But somehow Jonathan wasn't afraid. "We'll let them see us," he hissed excitedly. "If they say, 'Wait there,' we'll stay where we are. If they say, 'Come up to us,' we'll climb up. That'll be our sign that the Lord has given them into our hands."

The gorge was steep: they went feet first, slithering on their bottoms, grabbing at tussocks of grass and stunted shrubs to slow themselves down.

The sunlight raked across them. A shout went up from the Philistine camp, now high above.

Jonathan gripped his sword hilt and gritted his teeth as he looked up. A couple of well-aimed arrows would kill both of them in a single moment...

But the Philistine sentries were laughing at them. "I told you there were Hebrews quaking in every crevice. Look, they're coming out of their holes."

"Do you want to join us, little Hebrews? Some of your friends have."

"Come up here and we'll teach you a lesson."

That's the sign. Jonathan's heart beat fast—but then a kind of calm flooded him. This was it. This was it! The Lord had given the Philistines into the hands of Israel!

He started to climb.

Oren was right behind him. The rock was creased and

knobbly, but it crumbled in places under their eager hands. They kept on, spurred by the taunts of the Philistines above: a handhold here, a foothold there... By the time Jonathan heaved himself over the cliff edge, his hands and knees were dripping with blood. He didn't notice.

The Philistines were lounging by the sentry post. They kept on laughing right until the moment Jonathan staggered upright and began to run. Then they went quiet; but it was too late. The long shaft of his spear quivered as the point drove into the heart of the nearest man. The Philistines scrambled for their weapons, but Oren was on them with his knife, hacking and stabbing; Jonathan raised his sword and dived past him.

"Israel!" they cried at the tops of their lungs. "ISRAEL!"

It was after that—after they'd attacked, and all the Philistines had scattered or been slain—that the earthquake struck.

CHAPTER 10

The Oath

"The earthquake has sent the Philistines into disarray," said one of the lookouts, slapping the trunk of the pomegranate tree beside Saul's chair. "The Lord is with us after all!"

"No," said the other lookout— "I mean, yes, of course, the Lord is with us—but they were in confusion already. I saw it just before the shaking started. I'm sure I did." He was leaning forwards in his excitement. "Something else must have alarmed them. I think… I think they must have been attacked."

"Without orders?" Saul's mouth twisted angrily. "Muster all our forces," he said to Abner, waiting beside him. "See who has left us."

Abner nodded and paced away towards the farm. Saul turned back to the two lookouts. "So you think they are ripe for attack."

"We should hurry," said the first man firmly. "They're

melting away already. If we want to destroy them we must act fast."

"Praise be to God!" breathed the second lookout. "Little did we think—"

"Yes," snapped Saul impatiently, "but go and find the priest. We must be sure of what the Lord wants."

"I'll go." Michal produced herself from behind the pomegranate tree.

"Still here?" said Saul in displeasure. "I told you to go—"

"Home, yes, I will, but I think the priest is there—I'll fetch him," she cried, already running away.

Saul watched his daughter dart between the groups of fighters already making their way up from the farm. She was not obedient, but at least she was fast… Unlike thick-set Abner, who was returning slowly: he could see him behind the other men, making no attempt to push past.

Eventually Abner arrived. "All the men are here," he told Saul, "except two." He hesitated; it was unlike him.

"Who?" said Saul with a frown.

"Jonathan," answered his cousin. "And Oren, his armour-bearer."

Saul kept his face blank. So. Jonathan and his little friend had attacked the Philistines, all on their own, and somehow sent them into retreat.

There was only one explanation: the Lord had been with them. The Lord had helped them, just like he'd helped Saul himself at Jabesh Gilead.

That meant…

Saul shook his head. He would have to think more about this later.

The priest ran up, the jewels in his linen breastplate rattling against their settings of gold. "Sir," he said breathlessly.

"Should we attack?" asked Saul. "I want to know."

"Should we—"

"Hurry, man," snapped Saul.

The priest began to fumble with his garments. "I need a little time—it is a serious thing to enquire of the Lord…"

Then a new messenger burst through the branches of the pomegranate tree. "They're fighting each other more and more," he cried. "They're ours for the taking."

"Saul," said Abner urgently, "surely the earthquake was sign enough."

Saul hesitated.

His eyes scanned the crowd of waiting men: their poor clothes, their worn-out shoes, their motley collection of mattocks and sickles and sharpened gardening forks. Forks, for goodness' sake. And there were so few of them, and there were so many Philistines—even if they were in retreat.

The men looked tired, weighed down by the long months holed up here in Gibeah hearing bad news. He himself felt as worn out as an old wineskin, and dirtier. But the soldiers' gaze on him was eager, hungry. *A king to lead us...* That was what they'd wanted three years before. That was what they needed now. Lord or no Lord.

His spear was leaning against the tree. He took it in his hand. "I will win vengeance against my enemies," he said vehemently. "But you must be devoted to this fight." He pointed his spear at them, meeting their eyes one by one. "Cursed be anyone who eats food—who eats anything at all—before evening comes. Cursed be anyone who stops to eat before I have avenged myself on my enemies!"

Then he raised his spear aloft, and shook his fist, and all of them yelled his name.

Jonathan paced through the trees. He and Oren had joined up with the rest of the army that morning; now, only a few hours past noon, they were well beyond Michmash, deep into Ephraimite territory. Here the woods were thick and the trees' looping branches were close together. Bees thrummed above Jonathan's head and he felt a pang of hunger. Smooth, sweet honey, spooned over warm fluffy bread... oh, if only...

But the battle wasn't over yet.

They could do it: they could really rid the land of Philistines altogether. There'd been Israelites in the Philistine army who'd turned and started fighting on the right side once the panic started. And there'd been Israelites hiding in the hills who'd risen up to join Saul's army as it swept past Michmash—*coming out of their holes,* Jonathan thought, remembering the words of the Philistine sentry with a grim smile. Who knew how many fighters exactly they had now? The woods were dense and they were spread out widely. But there were enough.

If they pressed on. Stepping warily over a tree branch, Jonathan glanced at the men on his right and left. Weariness had dulled their eyes and made their faces sag. The day had been long, long, long.

Movement blurred beyond the man on the left and Jonathan cried out in warning—but it was too late: the Philistine had cut the man down. Jonathan leaped towards the killer. With a twist of his sword he pushed the weapon out of the man's hand—but the Philistine gave a roar and launched himself forward anyway. He was grabbing at Jonathan's tunic and pulling him down to the ground... They rolled in the dirt, thorns catching at their clothes and ripping their skin. Jonathan had lost his sword but he pummelled his enemy with punches—he was going to get free—the man's hands weren't gripping his body anymore...

Then he realised what the Philistine was doing. His grasping hands reached for Jonathan's face, grabbed him by the ears... He tried to jerk back, but the man had him fast. A big tree root rushed to the corner of his vision. Black pain descended as the man dashed Jonathan's head against it.

But Jonathan was still fighting. His flailing hand touched something cold—it was his sword, lying on the ground, just within reach. He grabbed it, barely feeling the sharp edges cut into his palm, and thwacked it as hard as he could against the man's side. The Philistine let go in surprise and Jonathan scrambled back, managing to get the sword-hilt properly in his hand. He hefted the blade and dived forwards. He felt it plunge deep into the man's soft flesh.

The body went limp. With a grunt Jonathan pushed him off and staggered away.

That had been close. He was tired, too tired... He retched suddenly and bent against a tree, but his stomach was empty; there was nothing to throw up. There was a long, straight stick on the ground; wearily he picked it up and propped it under one arm.

Something dripped on his neck. Was it blood? he wondered dimly. No, it was... it was honey. There was a pool of it on the ground, sputtering down from a branch above. He lifted his head and saw the bees busy on the honeycomb. Oh, it would be so delicious...

Leaning back against the tree trunk again, he raised his stick, sticking his tongue out as he concentrated. A little higher... a little higher... Yes! He'd reached it. The bees throbbed—he mustn't disturb them... Carefully he twisted the stick until the end of it was covered in honey. Then he lowered it again and put his trembling hand to the wood. The honey oozed over his fingers; he shoved them in his mouth like a tiny child, sucking it all in greedily.

"Sir!" A soldier was standing there; one of Jonathan's own men. He looked shocked.

Jonathan stood up properly, feeling better already. "What?"

"Your father's oath…" whispered the man, horrified.

Jonathan went cold. "What oath?" he said.

CHAPTER 11

Father and Son

Evening came. Saul stood on the last slope of the hill country, looking down over a wide grassy valley. Cows grazed in it peacefully, and there were sheep clustered in pens further down the hill. This was the edge of Israelite land; they'd driven the enemy out of Israel completely. They'd actually done it.

They had found the remnants of another Philistine camp. There were already Israelites stretching themselves out around newly rekindled fires, rummaging among the left-behind baggage, trying on abandoned armour for size. Saul felt a flash of irritation: they should have been awaiting his orders, not putting their feet up.

"Look!" someone said as they made their way into the camp. "They're eating!"

"That's all right," said someone else with a glance at Saul, "we've won, we can—"

"No," said the first man, "look, they're sinning against

the Lord. They're eating meat with the blood in it."

It was true: Saul spotted a sheep lying half-butchered on the grass just in front of him. Its head was at an odd angle and its wool was bright red with blood. There was a grisly heap of guts next to it. Saul turned aside with a wrinkled nose. Who had done this? It should have been slaughtered properly, the precious blood allowed to drain away. That was God's law.

Around the nearest fire there were men gobbling the meat. One pulled a fresh skewer of still-pink mutton from the flames and shoved it smoking into his mouth. Too fast: he howled in pain and spat out the meat. Its hot blood bubbled out from his gasping lips. Two other men tried to grab the skewer; they pushed the first man over as they fought, and then he joined in the fight too, tearing at their hair and kicking his legs up from his sprawled position on the ground. Eventually one of them won and ran off with the meat, crouching with his back turned like a jealous dog.

Was this what hunger did to them? Was this the result of the oath? Saul turned away, nostrils flared, and saw another little group of fighters, hacking and hacking at a fresh carcass. They stuck the chunks of meat on the skewers with shaking fingers, then half ran, half stumbled to the nearest fire.

Saul's legs were screaming with weariness, but he stamped towards the men and roared at them with all his might. "You have broken faith!" he cried, kicking one of them hard in the side before he had time to control himself. "You have broken faith!"

"We're starving!" one of them cried. "We've fought all day…"

But Saul ignored him.

"Bring me a stone!" he barked. "Bring the animals here and slaughter them properly. Do not sin against the Lord."

Look! he said grumpily in his own mind as they rolled a huge stone towards him, set it down, and then heaved the nearest dead sheep onto it. Blood began to drip out onto the ground. *Look!* thought Saul: *I'm making them obey you, Lord! That's what you want, isn't it? Will you let me stay king if I make them obey you?*

The men gathered around the stone with greedy eyes. Saul sat down next to it, folding his arms. "I'm hungry too," he said. "But we must wait."

Two hours later there were no more animals grazing in that part of the valley. The ground was soaked with blood. The men were full and happy. Saul sat aside from them, one elbow propped on his knee; he was trying to look kingly, but he felt cut off and lonely. The men blamed him for their hunger: he knew it. They wouldn't want him to join them.

Not so with Jonathan, though: Jonathan was right in the middle of them. He sat by a fire, surrounded by a ring of eager soldiers asking him question after question about the attack at Michmash. Saul could hear his son deflecting the men's praise, telling them enthusiastically that it was all the Lord's doing. His face was bright and animated. Saul's own features twisted bitterly.

He was glad of the darkness. It was ridiculous to be jealous of your own son.

He stood up. Where were Abner and the other captains? Oh, yes: over there. He jerked his head to summon them. The priest, too. Jonathan he left to his adoring listeners.

"What's the plan from here?" asked Abner as they gathered. "The men are ready to go on now, if you choose."

He did not say, *If you'd let them eat sooner we could have won half of Philistia by now,* but Saul did not fail to notice the impatience in his cousin's voice.

Saul set his feet a little wider. "Let's go down and pursue the Philistines by night," he said, trying to sound confident and brash. "We'll plunder them til dawn. We won't leave one of them alive."

Abner and the other captains exchanged glances. One of them shrugged. "Whatever seems best to you."

But the priest coughed in interruption. "Let us en-quire of God," he said, fingering the ephod at his waist.

Saul nodded. What difference would another small delay make? "Ask: Shall I go down and pursue the Phil-istines? Will God give them into Israel's hand?"

The priest rushed away down to the stream to wash. Returning, he straightened his garments and muttered in prayer. Then he thrust his hands into the ephod and brought out the stones. Saul held his breath…

The priest opened his hand. The Urim and Thummim sat on his palm. They were both blank.

"No answer," stammered the priest. "I'll try again—" But he tried three more times and each time the stones showed their uncarved faces.

At last Saul snarled, "Enough. He is not answering." He looked around at the gathered captains. "Someone must have done wrong. The Lord is displeased."

None of them answered.

"Let's find out what sin has been committed," Saul said angrily. Without meaning to, he glanced down the hill, towards the fires where his son still sat eagerly talking. He thought of Jonathan's escapade, just before the earthquake… He hadn't got to the bottom of that yet. He thought of his son's reluctance to let the sacrifices be made in Gilgal, his arrogance and lack of respect in front of all the commanders.

He wishes he were king instead of me, Saul thought. *He thinks he should be.*

A man after God's own heart, Samuel had said…

As he turned back to the captains again, Saul's eyes glittered. "As surely as the Lord who rescues Israel lives," he said slowly, "whoever is at fault must die. Even if the guilt lies with my son Jonathan, *he must die.*"

He saw the surprise in Abner's face, just for a moment; then his cousin looked down. Saul raised his eyebrows, waiting to see if any of the others would challenge him. But they didn't say a word.

Jonathan had never seen his father like this. He seemed full of quiet determination—but not in a good way. There was a kind of malice in the set of his jaw and the hardness of his eyes. Jonathan frowned, trying to shake off the strange sense of fear and foreboding that was gripping him.

The two of them, father and son, stood apart on the slope; the rest of the army was massed below. In between stood the priest.

"Why, O Lord," intoned Saul, "have you not answered your servant today? If the fault lies with me or my son Jonathan, respond with Urim; but if the men of Israel are at fault, respond with Thummim."

The priest drew the tokens from the ephod. He stretched out his hand. One of the stones lay face up, its deeply etched symbol clear and black against the white stone. Urim.

Jonathan swallowed.

The king spoke again in prayer. "If the fault lies with me, respond with Urim; if it is Jonathan, respond with Thummim."

The priest put the stones back in the ephod, washed

his hands again in a basin someone had found, and drew out the tokens one final time.

Thummim.

"Tell me," said Saul coldly, turning to Jonathan, "what you have done."

Jonathan stared at him, aghast.

He hadn't even *known* about the stupid oath!

"I tasted a little honey," he said, "with the end of my staff. And now—" he wanted to sound brave but he couldn't keep the sob out of his voice— "now I must *die?*"

Saul's gaze was perfectly steady. "Your sin has displeased God. Now we're too late to pursue the Philistines, and it's your fault. May God deal with me, be it ever so severely, if you do not die."

Jonathan's mouth was open: he felt like gasping for air. Numbly he remembered the attack in Michmash that morning, when the Lord had sent panic over the Philistines. Only that morning! And now he was going to die! Was that really what the Lord wanted? Surely, surely not...

He thought of Michal and his other siblings... He thought of Oren, and Kish... He thought of his future, his dreams of being anointed king, and doing it better than his father... None of that would happen now. None of it. And what would happen to Israel? Beloved Israel!

He felt a tear start from his eye as he turned his head to look down the slope. The men met his gaze. Their faces were full of compassion.

There was a moment of utter silence.

Then someone shouted, "Never!"

Jonathan saw the king spin round as the shouter marched forwards out of the crowd. "Should Jonathan die?" he cried, standing in front of him protectively. "The very man who has brought about this great deliverance in Israel? Never!"

Another man stepped forward, running up the slope and putting his hand on Jonathan's shoulder. "As surely as the Lord lives," he growled, "not a hair of his head shall fall to the ground. He did this today with God's help."

"You can't kill him!" cried another man. "He's the king of the future!"

Jonathan's last glimpse of his father that evening was of a white face, tight with anger and jealousy. Then more soldiers poured around him, and Saul was lost from view.

PART THREE

A Man After God's Own Heart

Eight years later

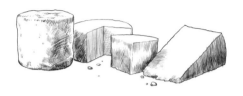

CHAPTER 12

Red Feathers

There was a hawk circling in the valley of Elah. Its wings were taut, its keen eyes tilted down towards the stream which stretched along the flat plain. It spotted something—a rat scuffling from shrub to shrub—and folded its wings, diving to earth as fast and strong as a well-aimed slingstone.

A youth on the hillside pulled his mule up short to watch. Yes! It had got its prey: it was flapping upwards again, the rat hanging from its yellow talons. Its wings beat in the clear air as it screamed in triumph.

Leaning back against his saddlebags, the youth watched the bird reach a tree on the far side of the valley. It disappeared from his sight; he turned his gaze lower, to the armies already gathering around the thin stream. On this side, the leather-clad army of Israel. The king and his captains were easy to pick out as the only men in proper armour; their bright figures rode between the lines as the men stepped into formation. On the other side, every Philistine's head was crowned with dark red feathers. From this distance they looked like a stream of blood, pouring down into Israel.

This valley had been green once.

"Lord," whispered the youth fervently, "may Israel be like that hawk. May the Philistines be like that rat."

Then he pressed his heels into his heavy-laden mule, and they made their way down the hill.

Saul had held onto the kingdom. He was, after all, the one who had driven the Philistines entirely out of Israelite land. The Lord must be with him, people had said.

And he liked to think he was a better king now. Stronger. He'd started making every clan and tribe pay taxes, and used the money to seek out the best warriors and pay them a wage so that they were always ready to fight. No one stood a chance of taking the kingdom away from him now—not easily, anyway. And Gibeah had become a proper royal town, fortified and wealthy. Saul had far more flocks than his father Kish had ever had.

Yes, he'd grown into kingship the way his middle son, Ishvi, had grown into Jonathan's hand-me-down tunics. Not that the boy had hand-me-downs anymore: only the best clothes hung from the backs of the royal princes. Yes. It didn't matter what Samuel had said. Saul didn't need him. He was the king.

Still, as the trumpets blew in the valley of Elah, there was a part of Saul that wished the prophet were there.

The men were all formed up into their lines now. The soldiers in the front rank were braced and ready. Behind them the archers had arrows notched to their bows. In any other place, in any other battle, Saul would have surveyed them with deep pride and confidence. But not today.

His body tensed as he heard the familiar heavy footsteps crunching on the other side of the stream. The huge spear tapping against the bronze greaves. The ripple of the hundreds of metal scales that covered Goliath's body like the skin of a snake.

Goliath! Goliath the giant! Saul turned to watch him, his stomach grisly and grey. He tried to keep his face expressionless as the champion of the Philistines began to shout.

"Why do you come out and line up for battle?" Goliath bellowed jeeringly. "I defy the armies of Israel! Choose a man and let him fight me!"

He was taller than anyone, far taller than Saul, and armoured from head to foot. His beard was dyed red to match his countrymen's feathers. His shield-bearer scurried alongside him like a mangy bird following a huge ox.

The front ranks held their spears steady. Saul saw more than one pair of white eyes flick to him and Abner, on horseback at the end of the line; then flick forwards again, full of fear.

He'd lost count of the days that Goliath had paced up and down the lines, taunting the Israelites with his challenge. The two armies were evenly matched: neither could attack the other without heavy losses. This Goliath was the Philistines' solution.

"If your man kills me, the Philistines surrender!" he'd thundered, day after day. "If I kill him, you do! Choose a man and let him fight!"

But no man had been chosen. No man had volunteered.

If Samuel were here... But Saul pushed the thought away. Samuel wanted nothing more to do with him; he'd made that very clear. Anger surged within Saul as he thought about it—but once again he pushed the feeling away. He was getting better now at controlling the fits of rage that had begun to seize him ever since his last meeting with the prophet. He shifted in his seat, breathing in, breathing out. *I am the king.*

But Goliath still paced on the plain, and sooner or later someone would have to fight him.

When the youth rode into the camp, the keeper of supplies recognised him at once. "Back again, David?" he called cheerfully. "Your father let you out?"

David grinned as he unloaded his heavy sacks of grain and bread and yellow cheese. "Lamb time's over," he said. "Here, I brought this for my brothers."

"I'll see they get—" But the youth had already sprinted away, down towards the battle lines.

The keeper of supplies shook his head as he took the
mule's reins and led him away. He stroked the animal's
nose. "That boy… What will become of him, hmm?"

David knew where to go. He flew down the hill and
slipped through the lines of men, his small frame finding space between the spears and shields. He found his
brothers quickly: they were in their usual place.

"What's happening?" he asked breathlessly. "Why
aren't we fighting?"

"We?" said Eliab, the oldest. "You're not part of this
army."

"Not because I don't want to be."

He'd come down here with Saul originally—he was
one of the king's attendants—but when the army mus-
tered, David's father had insisted that he go home and
keep the sheep while his older brothers fought.

Except that they still hadn't actually fought.

"What's happening?" David asked again, standing on
tiptoe to try to see past the mass of bodies all around
them.

"Goliath," answered Eliab, and filled him in.

David was quiet for a moment. "So, nobody's brave
enough to fight the enemy of the Lord."

Eliab rolled his eyes. "Don't start, David. You don't
understand—"

But the youth was already pulling at the sleeve of the

man in front of him. "What will be done," he asked, "for the man who kills this Philistine and removes this disgrace from Israel?"

The man turned. He looked down. He laughed in surprise. Then his brow furrowed as he saw the glint in David's eyes and realised he was serious. "The king will give him great wealth, and his daughter's hand in marriage," he said.

David nodded.

"David—" said Eliab warningly—but it was too late.

"Who is this Philistine?" the youth said stormily. "What gave him the right to defy the armies of the living God?"

Eliab grabbed his arm. "Why did you come down here?" he hissed. "You arrogant kid."

But David had wriggled from his brother's grip. "Can't I even speak?"

He didn't hear the rest of Eliab's words; he was already walking away down the line.

CHAPTER 13

Not Just a Sheep-Boy

"*Why did you come down here?*" He should have known Eliab would react that way. David had spent half the spring shuttling back and forth between the army in Elah and the farm back in Bethlehem, trying to do his duty by both his father and the king. The sheep at home needed looking after, but Saul did too. David had lost count of the number of early mornings when he had swung his lyre over his shoulders and his legs over his mule's back and set off to the valley of Elah in the dark. Was it not fair enough that he wanted to see how the army was getting on? Couldn't he even ask a question without his brother calling him arrogant?

I don't want to be arrogant, he thought fiercely as he peered between the lines of soldiers, hunting for a better view of the giant Philistine. *I'm just trying to do what God wants.*

God had chosen Saul as king, so David had to serve him. And God had said in his law that you must honour your parents, so David had to keep his father's sheep.

And now, this Philistine… what would God say about *him*?

David had a feeling that he knew the answer to that question.

He caught sight of Saul seated on his horse at the end of the line. The king was too far away to see his face, but David could just imagine it: it would have a hard look, stony and unreadable, but behind the surface there would be a boiling torrent of anxiety. Or anger… You never quite knew with Saul.

In normal times—when they weren't at war, and when it wasn't lambing time—it was David's job to play his lyre and soothe the king whenever he was seized by rage. Saul's cousin Abner had pinned David against the wall last year when he'd first turned up in Gibeah and been given his duties: "No one is to know how bad the king gets," the commander growled, "do you understand? No one."

"I'm loyal to him, I promise," David had answered, gulping. "He's the Lord's anointed king."

Abner had rolled his eyes and let him go.

And David *was* loyal—not that that had ever mattered very much before. He was just a lad, a boy everyone liked but, he knew it, just a sheep boy and the youngest of eight sons. His father, Jesse, was not a particularly important or wealthy man and David had to earn his keep. He might live only half a day's journey from Gibeah, but his life had always been a world away from the goings-on of royalty.

Until Samuel had turned up.

David had been out in the hills with the sheep—this was a year or so ago, well before he'd gone to Gibeah to become the king's attendant. He'd been tuning his lyre while the sheep grazed, all peaceful beneath a green tree. Then he'd heard the slap of sandals on stone and seen one of his brothers haring towards him.

"You're wanted," Abinadab had said, and then, "You'd better wash." But there had been no more information; he'd just given David a shove and settled down in his place.

David had stared at him.

"Go on," his brother had said. "I'll watch the sheep. Go!"

So David had scurried away, and when he'd got home he'd found the table set out ready for a meal, and his father and all his other brothers standing around looking impatient, and Samuel in the middle of them.

The prophet was bent-bodied and white-bearded, his face as lined and pitted as a cliff. He'd looked at David very carefully, then stood up slowly, keeping his gaze on the youth the whole time.

Everyone else was looking at him too. David had never been more aware of the muddy stains on his tunic, the grazes on his knees and the red calluses on his fingers. And the smell of sheep, which no quick splash of water to the face was ever going to get rid of.

Samuel had a polished ox-horn in his hand, hollow and filled with something. With oil, David saw as the old prophet came towards him. Suddenly Samuel's withered hands were trembling over his head. The thick, fragrant oil was slipping over David's hair and running down his cheeks.

David shut his eyes and held his breath. Partly because of the oil, but partly also because it felt like something was happening—something tremendous...

"So this is the one the Lord has chosen? Out of all my sons?" His father's voice was confused, unbelieving. "He's a good lad, I'll give you that, but... Well, to put it frankly... Why him?"

Chosen? What for? David opened his eyes just a crack, in time to see Samuel shake his head.

"The Lord knows," was the prophet's only answer. But David could see a whole range of emotions in the old prophet's cloudy eyes. Pride, the way his mother looked at him; hope, like he saw in Eliab's face when the betting was going his way; and something else... a kind of sadness.

Then David's father had clapped his hands impressively, and they'd all had to sit down to eat. It was a feast—olives and fresh bread and boiled mutton all steaming and rich, and then honey cakes and pressed figs for after, and the best wine to wash it all down with—but David hadn't been hungry. He'd sat at the foot of the table, watching Samuel, wishing he could ask a thousand questions.

It was a few months after that that he'd been summoned to Gibeah to play his lyre for the king.

And yes, Saul had been... well, he hadn't been quite what David expected. But they had something in common—not that David would ever have dared to tell Saul that. They'd both been anointed by Samuel. Saul for kingship, and David for... for something. David had seen the seriousness in Samuel's eyes, and he knew God didn't make mistakes. Saul was the king, and that was that, however out of control he got.

But what was Saul going to do about Goliath?

"This is the lad. The one who's been sounding off about fighting the Philistine."

Jonathan looked up at Abner's words. The commander muscled into the royal tent, pulling a young man with him—a boy really, in a dirty tunic and travel-worn sandals. As Abner let go of him, the youth bowed and smiled to all the captains crowded into the tent. He stepped towards Saul and knelt respectfully to the ground. "My king," he said.

Jonathan watched him curiously. He looked like a shepherd, not a warrior: his bare arms were muscly but he was small and fresh-faced. As he stood up Jonathan spotted a graze on his knee.

Jonathan's gaze slid to Ishvi, his younger brother, comparing the two. Ishvi was older, but not stronger... And the prince was pale and sullen, while this boy was smiling all round him. He looked like he was at a sheep fair ready to spend his spare change. Jonathan would have laughed if he hadn't already been frowning. The youth looked familiar... Where had he seen him before?

"It's David," said Ishvi suddenly. "It is, isn't it? You're one of my father's lyre players, aren't you?"

David nodded happily. "I'm glad to be back with the king," he said.

Glad to be with the king? Jonathan folded his arms, frowning. What was this boy about? He'd come to see his brothers, Abner had said... He wasn't even part of the army. He'd found his way into the battle-lines and then started going on about defeating the Philistine champion. He was a fool, a show-off. A mere lad.

A mere lad? I was defeating Philistines when I wasn't much older. The words whispered themselves into Jonathan's mind. He shook his head slightly. *That wasn't the same.*

"So," Saul was saying expressionlessly, "You have been asking anyone you can find what I will do for the man who kills Goliath."

David nodded. "Let's not lose heart over this Philistine," he said lightly. "Your servant will go and fight him."

Saul laughed. He looked around, inviting everyone to share the joke, but their faces were grim: this was no time for jests. Saul refocused on David. "You can't go out against this warrior," he said. "You're only young."

David bowed his head. "Sir, your servant has been keeping his father's sheep recently."

I knew it. A sheep boy, thought Jonathan darkly.

"Sometimes a lion or a bear has come and carried off an animal from the flock," David went on. His voice was still light: frank, reasonable. "I go after it, strike it, and rescue the sheep from its mouth. When it turns on me I seize it by the hair, strike it, and kill it." He did not move as he spoke, but Jonathan saw the muscles in the youth's arms twitch involuntarily. He was small, but stocky and determined-looking; Jonathan could believe he was telling the truth.

He looked him up and down again, narrowing his eyes.

Then David said, "This Philistine has defied the armies of the living God. The Lord who rescued me from the lion's paw will rescue me from him."

Jonathan swallowed.

He himself had said things like that once.

Saul was smiling. It was an ugly smile, a sneer really. "Then go," he said in a silken voice. "And the Lord be with you."

CHAPTER 14

Champion

"I can't wear this." David had seen the king put on this armour a hundred times, but he'd never thought anyone would make *him* try it. The coat of metal reached halfway down his shins and the helmet was so heavy it felt like his head would sink into his shoulders. He eased it off, wincing. "I'm not used to it."

The king did not hide his smirk as he took it back.

David unclasped the metal coat and handed that back too. "I can't wear a king's armour. I'll go as I am. A staff would be good; I'm used to that."

"Suit yourself." Saul waved a finger and one of the attendants stepped forwards with a staff. It was a good one: straight and well-weighted, with a gnarly knot at the top. David thumped it once on the ground, then gazed around at them all brightly. They all looked horrified. David knew why: they were convinced he'd be killed. But they were wrong. David felt only a flicker of fear. He knew what he was going to do.

The Lord will be with me, he thought as the war trumpets blew outside the tent. At least, he was pretty sure. The Lord was faithful to those who were faithful to him; that was what the priests always said. And standing around putting up with the jeering of this man Goliath was *not* being faithful to the Lord.

"Do you have a plan for when he loses?" David heard Abner whisper to Saul just ahead of him as they made their way downhill. But the king made no reply.

They were in the valley now. It was still hot, although the afternoon sun was moving lower and lower in the sky. The battle lines formed quickly; mutterings stirred in them. "Who's that behind Saul?" David heard. And then, "That lad's our champion? Heaven help us…"

The captains rode off to take their places among the men. Saul and Abner stayed to one side, as before. Their horses danced and snorted nervously.

David gripped his staff. In the other hand he had his sling: a long leather loop he'd made himself. His thumb stroked it where it wound around his palm.

Then he walked forwards, alone.

He had nothing in his mind now except the stream in front of him; the army at his back was irrelevant. He knelt by the water, thinking of the rat he'd seen the hawk carry away. *Like that,* he prayed, leaning forwards and spreading one searching hand over the streambed. Just as he'd hoped: there were good slingstones here. He chose five and put them in the pouch at his waist.

He looked up. The Philistine was already there, taller than ever now that he was closer up. He hadn't spotted David yet. He was striding towards the stream, getting ready to make his usual taunts...

Not today, David thought fiercely.

He stepped over the stream.

"WHAT?" The Philistine had seen him. "Am I a dog," he bellowed, "that you come after me with *sticks?*"

David held his ground as Goliath came closer. It was true, his staff was like a twig in comparison with the Philistine's huge spear. The giant had a massive sword strapped to his side, too, and a long javelin slung over his shoulders. He was like a mountain of metal.

Spittle was spraying over Goliath's scarlet beard as he cursed David, the Israelites in general, and the Lord their God... He was still striding closer. "Come here," he spat, "and I'll feed your flesh to the birds."

David took another step forward. He let his staff fall from his hand; he didn't need it now. He squared his shoulders and shouted to the Philistine, so loudly he thought he might lose his voice. "You come against me with a sword and spear and javelin, but I come against you in the name of the Lord Almighty!"

The Philistine was laughing. How dare he! David swallowed, moistened his lips, and yelled again: "The God of the armies of Israel! He's the one you've defied."

He was breathing heavily. He glared at Goliath,

meeting the giant's gaze even from this distance. "Today," he called out hoarsely, "the Lord will deliver you into my hands. I'll—I'll strike you down. I'll cut off your head!"

Goliath was still advancing. David stopped shouting and slowly began to unwind the sling from his hand. "This very day," he muttered, "I'll give the carcasses of the Philistine army to the birds and the wild animals."

He felt for the pouch by his side. There were the five stones: smooth, round, waiting. He breathed in warm air and breathed out fury. He punched the sky with his free fist. "The whole world will know that there is a God in Israel! Everyone here will know that it's not by the sword or the spear that the Lord saves. The battle is the Lord's! The battle is the Lord's, and he will give you all into our hands!"

There was no point in waiting any longer; his sandals pushed off the ground. He sprinted forwards, eyes fixed on the giant Philistine. Dimly he heard the shouted curses of the red-feathered army beyond him. Goliath's shield-bearer was off to one side, stepping backwards as David made his charge... Goliath was motionless, the huge sword ready in his vast fist.

With practised hands David pulled a stone from his pouch and slotted it into the sling. It was a good weight. He whirled it in his outstretched arm, faster and faster, his shoulder joint straining... He judged the moment...

The stone whistled through the still afternoon air.

David slowed his pace. His lungs were on fire. The sling slapped back onto his wrist and hung there limply. His other hand hovered at the stone pouch, ready to choose another…

But there was no need.

Goliath's bronze helmet protected his cheeks, his crown, the back of his neck… but not his forehead.

The stone had struck him right above the eyes.

He fell. He fell quickly, stumbling backwards and landing heavily on the dry ground. His leg twisted oddly underneath him. After that he did not move.

David was still running; he reached the Philistine before the shield-bearer could. The giant was dead. He was dead. His hand lay limp around his sword hilt. David grabbed it and heaved it into the air—it was longer and heavier than any sword he'd ever carried, but just at this moment he felt stronger than he'd ever felt—and sliced it down across Goliath's thick neck.

Just like a bear, he thought grimly. *Just like a rat.*

Then he stood back.

There was a moment of silence.

There came a thin, wordless cry, somewhere deep in the Philistines' ranks.

Then "ISRAEL!" roared the army at David's back, and all at once the valley of Elah thundered with pounding feet.

CHAPTER 15

A Deep Cut

Jonathan had caught David up fast and the two of them had led the charge neck and neck. They'd been a rushing tide driving the Philistines out. You couldn't fault David for bravery. And he did really know how to fight; you wouldn't have guessed it if you'd only known the quiet lyre player, or even the shepherd lad who fought with bears, but he'd slung the rest of his stones as he'd run and then grabbed a sword from one of the men he'd hit. Soon he'd been slashing and parrying with the best of them. Shoulder to shoulder they'd been, like brothers. Like with Oren in the old days, before he went off to get married.

Then Jonathan had fallen behind. He'd got a deep cut and he'd lost blood. David had whirled ahead, calling out instructions to the men, taking Jonathan's place as naturally as if he'd been born to it.

Jonathan gasped again with pain. He was slowing

down, he could feel it. He had to get back and rest. Here was the stream in the middle of the valley... there lay Goliath still, his grisly head grimacing at the sky. Birds were circling above... they'd feast this evening.

As Jonathan thought of David again, he felt as if something was squeezing at his heart. He could hardly understand what he was feeling: his head was heavy with the loss of blood... Was it happiness, or disappointment? Or something else?

He staggered on. He felt someone's hands around his shoulders... A cup was being lifted to his lips.

"Come on," a voice said gently, "nearly there."

He allowed himself to be led to his father's tent. They were dressing his arm properly, helping him into a warm robe. He lay down with his head on a soft pillow. The world blinked and guttered like a dying flame...

When he woke, the tent was full of people. Saul was standing there, uninjured and resplendent still in his armour, facing towards the tent's opening. One of the commanders sat beside him, drinking deeply from a horn cup. Men and women were rushing in and out bringing dressings for wounds and jugs of water. None of them were looking at Jonathan.

A clean tunic lay folded on a chair next to the bed, he noticed; his belt was neatly coiled on top of it. His bow and his sword were there, too. He'd lost his spear in the pursuit of the Philistines, he remembered.

There was a cup of water; he drank it greedily and sat

up, adjusting the robe they'd put on him before he slept. It was his favourite: soft and warm, deep red with a blue border. He hugged it round himself, then winced again as he remembered his arm.

He took in the scene properly. The commander on the chair was sprawling back now with closed eyes, his thirst quenched. Saul, meanwhile, looked anything but relaxed. He was rolling back and forth on his heels like a child who'd been told to stay there and not move. A servant had brought a tray of food, but he hadn't noticed it.

Jonathan felt his stomach growl and was just about to ask his father if he could take something from the tray, but then Abner came in. Behind him was David.

Saul stopped rocking. He stood up tall—he must have been two whole heads taller than David, Jonathan noticed. But David didn't need to be tall. His hands gripped a twist of red-dyed hair. From the hair swung the head of Goliath.

David dropped the head on the ground before the king and knelt to the floor. "I have killed the Philistine, lord."

Saul looked at the head. It had landed face down. The hair at the back was matted with blood and flies were already starting to buzz around it. Saul curled his lip in disgust: "Take it away. No, not you!"

David had made to get up, but he fell back on the floor again as one of the other attendants scooped up the head and hurried out with it at arm's length.

One of the other attendants... Jonathan smiled. David wouldn't be a mere attendant for much longer, he thought.

His heart squeezed again like it had on the way back from the battlefield—like it was being pressed. Suddenly Jonathan realised why. David... No, he *wasn't* going to be an attendant for much longer. He was going to be much, much more than that.

He saw it all: Saul's kingship *was* going to be taken away after all, and it wouldn't be him, Jonathan, who would succeed him. It would be this youth, graze-kneed and bear-scarred and simple-looking though he was. Jonathan had felt it in the battle... He'd felt it even beforehand, though he hadn't wanted to admit it. The Lord was with David. It was all perfectly plain.

Jonathan felt suddenly very old and very wise. He'd wondered earlier whether he was happy or disappointed, and it occurred to him that he was both. Disappointed because all his dreams had been dashed. But blisteringly, astonishingly happy, because it now seemed that those dreams had never really been important to begin with. There was something better...

A man after God's own heart, Samuel had said, years ago in Gilgal. And here he was.

David was still kneeling before the king. Saul hooked a finger under the youth's chin and lifted it up. "Whose son are you, young man?" His voice did not betray any anxiety, but Jonathan's heart raced: his father had worked it out too… *Whose son are you*—in other words, are you important enough to be a threat?

"I am the son of your servant Jesse of Bethlehem," David said.

Nobody they'd ever heard of. Jonathan could almost feel his father's relief. But Saul had missed the point: it didn't matter whose son David was. Families were important, but not as important as God.

David was getting up; Saul patted him on the shoulder and murmured something about speaking to him later. The king strode out of the tent.

Jonathan stood up.

David started when he saw him and began to bow, but Jonathan waved his hand to say no. With his good arm he pulled off his princely robe and walked towards him. Moving slowly, painfully, he arranged the robe over David's shoulders. Its long hem pooled on the ground.

"These too," Jonathan said, motioning to the tunic on the chair, the coiled belt and the sword and bow. He handed each one to the younger man. "These are yours now." Then he reached out and made their two hands into one fist.

They didn't need to exchange many words. Each knew what the other meant.

Then Jonathan felt heavy and faint again, and David helped him stumble back to bed.

CHAPTER 16

Not My Brother

"**M**ichal, come on, we're running out of time."

Who'd have an older sister? Michal rolled her eyes as she slid another thin bangle onto her wrist and shook her hand slightly to let it settle with the others. Too many? Not enough? She didn't wear jewellery very often.

"Michal!" Merab sounded annoyed now.

Let her wait, Michal thought, leaning forward to check her reflection again in the mirror. The dark kohl around her eyes made the brown irises look deeper and brighter. Tiny pieces of amber studded her earlobes, matching the honey-coloured shawl wrapped loosely over her hair. Yes, this would do. She picked up her tambourine and stalked out of the room, taking her time.

Merab was tapping her foot in the courtyard, one dark eyebrow arched. Michal brushed past her. "Shall we go, then?" she said sweetly.

Outside was a group of other women, the house

attendants and farm workers. They were all dressed in their best clothes; a few had tambourines or small goatskin drums, and one was clasping a lyre. Michal nodded at them all as Merab pushed past her and led the way towards Gibeah's main gate.

"They'll arrive from that direction," Merab said bossily, pointing south. "The messenger said they're almost here. If we don't hurry, they'll reach Gibeah before we've got any distance from the gate."

"I know," said Michal.

"Well, why aren't you hurrying, then? Anyone would think you were just on your way to market. You haven't seen your father or brothers for *months*!" Merab was talking fast but, Michal noticed, not actually picking up her walking pace. "We need to celebrate them!" she went on. "They're heroes!"

"What about David?" asked one of the older women eagerly, a solidly built farm worker named Noa. "The new champion—will he be with them?"

"I expect so," answered Michal gloomily. It was Jonathan she wanted to see, not some muscle man who could think of nothing but war. That was how she imagined him, this champion who seemed to be the winner of every battle and skirmish of the summer: he'd have well-oiled hair and a flashy smile and no more than two sentences to string together. Either that or he'd be some grizzled old campaigner with knobbly veins in his arms. Ugh.

One of the more recent messengers had winked at her

and Merab and told them that Saul had promised this slayer of Philistines his daughter's hand in marriage. They'd sent the man straight out of the house, then avoided each other's gaze.

"That'll be you, then," Michal had said eventually. "You're the oldest."

"And the prettiest," Merab had shot back, and flounced away.

Secretly Michal hoped all these reports of David's successes were just hearsay: he'd won one or two battles, maybe, and people had got overexcited. He'd be a limping gap-toothed man who'd wormed his way into the king's favour by getting lucky once or twice. Michal had met more than one man like that among Saul's captains and retainers. A few more blows to the head in battle and David would be good for nothing—but Merab would still have to marry him, and she'd have to stop being so superior.

She would have one advantage over Michal if she did get married, though: she'd be out of Saul's house.

"Have you heard the song people are singing?" Noa asked. She sang it: "*Saul has slain his thousands, and David his tens of thousands.*"

Her voice had a husky, pleasant tone, and Michal smiled—until the words sank in. *Saul has slain his thousands, and David his tens of thousands.*

She stopped walking.

Merab had heard it too. "You can't sing that!" she

said, shocked. "That makes it sound like—like—" she lowered her voice— "like David is better than the king!"

Michal smirked. "Why not sing it," she said, "if it's true?"

Noa's eyes went from one sister to the other. "That's just what people are singing," she said, shrugging. "I can't help it."

"Well, we're not singing that today," said Merab.

They walked on. They were at the gate now; a crowd of other women were waiting there, children too. There were more musical instruments in their hands.

"Everyone ready?" said Merab brightly. "Dancers first, I think, and then drums. You with the lyres, you can walk alongside."

They turned around and set off out of the city again, downhill and south. Saul and his soldiers had come up through the territory of Judah; that was where David was from. No wonder they'd been singing songs in his honour there. But yes, Michal reflected as she began to dance along the road, it would really be more appropriate to praise the king more highly than his servant...

The sun caught at something shiny in the road up ahead. Was it them? Yes, they were coming down the hill: the first spear-tips were winking in the light... Michal clapped her hands in unison with the other dancers, stepping gracefully from side to side, dipping her head. She felt a special thrill as she raised her eyes again and saw the first figures coming towards them. Soon she'd see Jonathan!

Saul was on horseback at the front. Abner was beside him, as always. Jonathan must be on foot… Yes, there were two young men marching right behind the horses. Jonathan and Ishvi. Michal exchanged a happy glance with Merab, feeling a sudden rush of warmth. Merab wasn't so bad… soon they would all be together again…

Now that the men were in earshot, the women began to sing. Noa led them: "The king, the king," she sang. "The Lord gives victory to his anointed. The king rejoices in his strength!" They sang the words over and over, the lyre players picking out the tune. Michal raised her tambourine above her head, her bangles slipping down her arm. "The king, the king," she sang happily.

The two groups met; Saul was smiling and nodding. The women formed lines on either side of the column of marching men, like they'd planned. Michal wanted to make sure she wasn't too far from her brothers. She made one of the farm girls move aside and slotted herself into place. Then she turned to Jonathan and Ishvi, her tambourine rattling in her hand—

She stopped it dead. That wasn't her brother.

Jonathan was there, his eyes shining as he met her gaze—he had a new scar on his cheek and a poorer robe than usual but otherwise he looked the same as always, her own beloved brother. But Ishvi wasn't the one marching alongside him.

Michal dipped and danced to hide her confusion, her feet stamping confidently on the ground in time with the women in front and behind. She stole another look. The young man was grinning at her; his face was open and youthful… Wasn't that one of Saul's attendants? The lyre player? Michal frowned in disappointment. Maybe he'd become Jonathan's armour-bearer… But even so he had no right to be marching at the front, beside the prince.

And where was this champion, this David? Perhaps he'd stayed in Judah after all.

"Michal, Michal, it's good to see you," Jonathan was saying. But Michal glared at him coldly and then snapped her gaze away.

Later she regretted it. There were long tables laid out in the yard, covered with food; a sacrifice had been made to thank God for the victories of the summer, and then they'd all fallen to feasting. Jonathan had been home half a day by now and she hadn't spoken to him once.

She watched him curiously from across the yard. She hadn't seen him like this for a long time: relaxed, happy, no stiffness or bitterness to him. He was laughing with the lyre player, pointing out things and people to him; the youth was looking around with a smile. He had big eyes and a simple-looking face. A good-looking one, though, Michal admitted to herself. And a tuneful voice, she remembered.

A servant came up to the two young men, kneeling before them. He said something to the lyre player, who flushed, looking embarrassed. The man stood up again and went away, and Jonathan punched his friend lightly on the arm, laughing.

Michal frowned, feeling left out even though she was sitting on the opposite side of the yard.

Then Jonathan caught her eye. He lifted his eyebrows: *Want to come over here?*

Cross and pleased and embarrassed all at the same time, she glided towards them. Both of them stood up. Jonathan gave her a questioning smile: *Everything all right?* He touched her bare arm hesitantly. She wriggled in pleasure despite herself, gave up being stately, and clutched him in a hug.

"Michal," he said seriously, once they'd let go of each other, "I want you to meet—I want to introduce you to my friend. David."

The lyre player inclined his head again.

Michal stared. "David? You're David?"

Jonathan grinned, nudging his shoulder against his friend's. "You've heard of him, then?"

"You're the one who killed that Philistine?" She couldn't believe it. "You're the one who won all those battles?"

He wrinkled his nose. "I'm afraid so."

"With the Lord's help," Jonathan said in a proud voice.

Michal didn't know what to say. She felt small suddenly,

and foolish. What had she been doing? She rubbed her arm as if she were cold, biting her lip. The boy was looking at her with concern. She dropped her gaze, mumbled something, and fled away.

She went to her own room, pulled the bangles angrily from her wrists, and curled up on her bed, hiding her face. She pressed her hand into her chest and felt her heart beating deep inside her.

She didn't want Merab to be the one to marry that boy.

PART FOUR

Enemies

Four years later

CHAPTER 17

Then He Ran

"Son." Saul stood up with a smile as Jonathan came in. "What's the news?"

"We won again." Jonathan bowed. His hair was dusty from the road, Saul saw; but he looked well. Saul put his arm around his son's shoulders, ushering him to a table where bowls of fat grapes and a flagon of cool wine waited.

Jonathan drank deeply. "Completely defeated," he said. "I hope that'll be the end of them."

"We'll see," Saul answered. He felt relaxed and indulgent; who cared if the Philistines kept attacking? For now it was good that his son was back from the battle, safe and sound.

"Will you see to the feast?" he asked Jonathan. "It'll be new moon soon; we can celebrate the victory then. You'll take the best seat, of course."

"Yes, Father." But Jonathan's face creased slightly.

What was the matter? Saul patted his son on the shoulder. "What's worrying you?"

Jonathan hesitated. Then he said, "It was David's victory really."

Saul withdrew his hand.

David's victory. Again.

Jonathan started to describe David's brilliant battle tactics and the admiration he inspired among the troops. Suddenly Saul didn't feel so relaxed. He cut in hurriedly: "Of course, of course. David will sit by my side at the feast. The seat of honour. Of course." He patted Jonathan's shoulder again, less gently this time. "Go and rest. You can give me a proper report later."

Jonathan bowed again and retreated, popping one last grape into his mouth as he went.

Saul sat down. He stared at the wall. He tried to empty his mind of all its swirl of thoughts...

Then the music started.

It was coming through the wall. A few notes at first, one high, one low... then chords as several strings were struck at once by the lyre player's fingers.

David's fingers.

Saul cursed.

Soon the boy would start *singing*.

The king closed his eyes, breathing deeply. He'd loved David's music at first. Loved *him*: his open face, his quick smile... there was something simple and soothing about the son of Jesse.

But gradually, gradually, he'd realised that David's simplicity was all just a lie.

It must be. He must have some secret motive. Otherwise, why would he win all those battles and then refuse any kind of reward? It made no sense. The boy had even refused to marry Merab when he'd been offered her: "Who am I, that I should be son-in-law to the king?" he said, shaking his head deferentially any time it was mentioned. As if he was just the stinking shepherd he'd started off as. So *humble...* It could only be fake. There had to be something else David wanted.

The lyre got louder in the next room. Stopped. Started again. David's voice muttered dimly. He must be writing songs.

Saul fingered his spear.

The boy had married Michal in the end. Saul had always thought there was something odd about the fact that he'd agreed to *that* marriage without hesitation. And it was plain that Michal now loved David more than she loved Saul. More than her own father! More than the *king*!

Then there was Jonathan, whose eyes lit up every time he saw David coming.

Pah. Did David think he had Saul fooled? He was plotting something. He was using Saul's own children against him. Yes... David wanted Jonathan and Michal to turn away from their father! He wanted *everyone* to turn away from Saul and follow him instead. Yes... that had to be it.

Saul stood up abruptly. David wanted to get rid of him. That was the only explanation. *David wanted to be the king.*

"But God chose *me*." Saul's voice was a low hiss. "*I* am the king!"

He felt the weight of his spear. It was a good one, a well-balanced shaft of ash with a sleek, sharp spearhead. He hadn't used it yet. He swung it over his head then lunged forward, testing it. *Still limber, still fit,* he thought as he bounced onto his toes, breathing deeply. *Still king.*

He was a *good* king: he'd brought wealth and strength to Israel. He'd led them into battle like they wanted. It was true that there were still thieves in the towns and bandits on the roads and all the rest of it, but what was he supposed to do about that, really? And people still made their sacrifices to the Lord and didn't worship false gods, and frankly Saul thought the Lord ought to count that as a success.

Words floated through from next door, accompanied by a proper tune now. Something about God, of course. Saul stiffened despite himself, as if the words could hurt him.

"The Lord is righteous,
he loves justice,
the upright will see his face."

See his face, indeed. Saul's own face twisted. The boy sang about God like he *knew* him.

He gripped his spear again and took a step towards the door, heart beating. He'd had enough. He'd finally had enough. He'd tried to have David killed once before but Jonathan had come in all full of charm and smiles and talked him out of it.

I was a fool to listen to him. The thought growled into Saul's mind. There was no getting away from it. *I am a fool if I let this boy live.*

He wrenched open the door. His hands were shaking: he squeezed them around the new spear, willing himself to become like the cool metal at its tip—cold, smooth, effective. "The kingdom is *mine*," he hissed, as if the words could steady him. He stepped forward. The next room had only a curtain over the doorway. He put out his hand, careful, careful, ready to tear it aside…

His fingers pulled the fabric away. On the other side of the room, David looked up. That innocent face! Those wide eyes! Saul boiled with hate—he'd had enough—he never wanted to see the boy again—he wanted to kill him—he wanted to punch him until he was dead—he wanted to see him *bleed…*

Saul hurled his spear.

David dived aside. The spear struck the wall where the boy's head had been a second before and fell to the ground in pieces. David snatched up his lyre and ran for it.

Saul knelt, his hands flat on the floor, breathing in and out.

He's escaped. He's escaped, was the only thought in his boiling mind.

Then he got to his feet.

No, he told himself. David hadn't escaped. Not yet.

David clutched the lyre to his chest as he ran. Its strings cut into his palm. The pain was helpful, reminding him that this was really real, it wasn't a dream, that spear really had come within a finger's breadth of his head, and now he really had to run...

It wasn't the first time Saul had thrown a spear at him, but it was the first time it had felt so much like he meant it.

David shook himself: he had to think about where he was going. Automatically his feet were taking him homeward. Was that right? Yes... he wanted Michal. He wanted to be in the snug stone house the two of them shared right at the edge of Gibeah, where the window of its upper room looked out onto the green hills... He wanted to be safe.

You're kidding yourself, said a voice in his head. But he pushed the thought away.

He'd got well away from Saul's house by now. He slowed his pace, unsticking the lyre from his hand, wincing as the strings came away. He held it by its frame instead, more lightly, as if he were just wandering from one room to another.

He felt calmer. It was all right. He'd escaped. Saul hadn't really meant it, surely. He did things like that, angry things just on impulse. He'd be calmer now already. He wouldn't come after him.

Here was Gibeah's main gate: David was still within sight of Saul's house. Without really thinking about it he moved into the shadows. Back down the hill one of the king's servants was lighting torches; darkness was already falling.

A man stepped into the torchlight. Another followed him. The edges of their swords gleamed silvery white.

David drew in his breath.

Then he ran.

He whirled around the gatepost and into the town. If only his house were closer to the gate! Gibeah was still filled with people: the darkness wasn't deep enough yet to keep them indoors… He wished he were on the other side of his own barred door, that wonderfully thick wood…

"Evening," said someone, a neighbour. "Everything all—"

"Got to get home," David cut across him with a forced laugh, "my belly's howling!" He patted the man on the shoulder as he passed. Yes, he had to seem normal. It wouldn't help if people thought he'd fallen out with Saul.

He was walking quickly. He could see his own door… Inside there'd be quietness and safety, at least of a kind.

A little fortress all of his own. The window, and the dark quiet hills.

Were the men still following? Surely, but he didn't dare turn round. He reached the door. His hand felt the smooth wood. He lifted the latch, opened it. He was inside, the door was closed, the bar was firm and thick across it...

He sank to the floor, wobbly. *Come on, David,* he chided himself, *you're never scared. You've faced thousands of enemies.*

But none of those enemies had been the king himself.

A Rope from the Window

Michal felt as if her heart would break into pieces.
"You have to go," she said, staring into David's
face. She leaned forward and gripped his knees and said
it again: "You have to go *now*. If you don't run tonight,
tomorrow you'll be killed."

"I don't—"

"I know, you don't want to run, you're not a scaredy
bird, the Lord will keep you safe, you rely on him, but
David, my father is out for your blood. Maybe the Lord
plans to keep you safe *somewhere else*. In Gibeah your
time is up."

David curled his fingers around hers, biting his lip,
still hesitant.

How could she make him see? Michal pulled her
hands away, buried her face in them. "David, he's got
men *right outside the door* waiting for you to put one
toe out. Look, I know that my father is the Lord's

anointed. God chose him to be king. But that doesn't mean you have to just sit here and take everything he throws at you." She clutched at him again suddenly, digging her nails in. "It doesn't mean you have to let him kill you."

The two of them stared at each other. The fire crackled, throwing shadows on the wall; for a moment David's face went dark. Then it was lit again by the warm orange light.

"You're right," he said simply. "What shall I do?"

"You can escape out of the window. Go to Samuel," Michal replied. She stood up and started pulling out baskets, finding clothes and blankets... what would he need? How could she know?

She had an idea: "I'll bake you some bread," she told him. "I'll make it fast—it'll be like when our ancestors left Egypt, all in a hurry—"

"Bread without yeast, no time to let it rise," he smiled, "and they escaped, and God brought them here, to the promised land, to be his people."

She was right: the thought of it had comforted him. She kissed his cheek. "Get whatever else you need."

By the time she'd finished cooking he had a small bag ready; she wrapped the hot flatbreads in a scrap of cloth and stuffed them in the top. Then she let some rope down out of the window. The hillside dropped sharply down from the base of the wall; it was a good thing they lived right at the edge of town.

"I'll put something in the bed," she said hurriedly, choking back a sob, "some goatskin or something, so that when they come looking they'll think it's you. It'll buy you some time." Her hair had come loose; she was trying not to cry. "Oh, be safe, be safe."

He put out a hand and tucked her hair carefully behind her ear. This time she couldn't stop the sob from coming out. She flung her arms around him, squeezing him tight, not wanting to let him go.

"Be safe," she whispered.

"Samuel will help me," he replied quietly. "You're right. And the Lord. I've done nothing wrong. He'll keep me safe. He's my helper. Better than walls." Gently he pulled her arms away from his waist, setting them by her sides. He kissed her, just once. "My helper. My fortress. Yours too, Michal."

Then he climbed out of the window and was gone.

She woke with a dry mouth and a twisting feeling in her stomach. It was early; outside, the hills were still muffled in darkness.

Beside her lay the little statue, wrapped in the rumpled bedclothes. She flinched away from it in disgust, even though she was the one who'd put it there. She'd done it late last night, in case her father's men forced their way in while she was still sleeping. It was far smaller than David and the scrap of goatskin she'd arranged like hair on its head didn't look anything like his soft curls. But it might make them pause—it might trick them for a day or two. She could say he was ill and they weren't to come any closer.

She groaned as she got out of bed, rubbing her arms to warm herself up. The room was big and empty. There was still no light coming through the window.

The stones under her feet were cold as she tiptoed gingerly downstairs into the little courtyard at the centre of the house. The sky loomed above her. It was beginning to lighten at last, although there were still a few stars. She wondered where David was, and if he could see them too.

There was the door. Michal pressed herself against it, listening. She held herself very still even though her bare toes were screaming with cold. All her muscles were tense. But were her father's thugs still there?

For a long time there was no noise. At last Michal began to peel herself away from the door. Her toes curled in anticipation of a lit fire, shoes—

Then there was a cough, and a shuffle, and one gruff voice followed by another.

"Ready?"

"Yes. It's time."

Michal sprang back as the men outside thumped heavily on the door. Her elbow banged painfully against the wall. Clutching it, trying not to make a sound, she scurried back up the stone steps and threw herself in a ball on the floor, gasping, willing them to go away.

But they didn't.

"Open up! Open up in the name of the king!"

The king. The king. *The Lord is king,* David always said… He'd be her helper.

She had to be brave.

Michal stood up. Holding her head high, ignoring her cut elbow and her freezing toes, she walked slowly down the stairs and lifted the heavy bar away from the door.

She recognised the men. They'd been boys when she first knew them, playing with shiny stones in the dirt. They'd grown into ugly men, whom Saul used to do ugly jobs.

She raised an eyebrow.

"We've come from your father," said one of them, looking a little embarrassed.

"We're after the son of Jesse," said the other, more roughly.

Could they not even call David by his own name? "My husband, the king's son-in-law, is unwell," answered Michal crisply. "He cannot come just now."

"Ill," said the first man worriedly, "er…"

"Ill, is he," growled the second. "I'd like to see that for myself."

He made to step across the threshold, but Michal eyeballed him. "Has the king, my father, actually instructed you to break into my house? Please!" She rolled her eyes derisively. "My husband is in bed and looks likely to remain there some time. I should be tending to him. Tell the king we will both see him when David is better."

Then she closed the door in their faces.

But they were soon back. This time Michal found herself being pushed aside: "The king says, bring him to the palace in his bed if we have to."

"That's ridiculous—"

But they were already halfway up the stairs.

Michal waited at the bottom, knowing what would happen. They'd go to the bed. They'd find the stupid statue. They'd know she was lying. They'd tell her father.

She gripped her cut elbow so tightly her fingers went white.

When the men reappeared they were leering at her, knowing they had the upper hand.

"Think you'd better come and tell the king the truth, don't you?"

They tried to grab hold of her then, but she shook them off. "Remember who I am," she said coldly, then marched outside of her own accord, bare feet and all.

She did regret the bare feet a bit as she made her way to the house where she'd grown up. The road was sharp with stones and sticky with—well, it was better not to think about it. But she betrayed no flicker of emotion as she walked; nothing except cold disdain.

Her father was pacing up and down outside the house, his face mottled red with rage.

"Where is he?" he cried as they drew near. "Where is that traitor?"

"Gone," said the men grimly, and they explained what they'd found in David's bed.

Michal watched her father become very still. He turned his eyes on her. They were expressionless now, like a snake's. Michal flinched, half expecting a forked tongue to slither out of her father's mouth.

Instead he hissed, *"What have you done?"* and lunged at her.

He had her by the wrist; his grip was too strong... *He'll kill me,* came the thought into Michal's mind...

Was God her fortress? Not right now, it seemed. She was going to have to look after herself, and there was only one thing she could think of to do.

She burst into tears.

"First him," she sobbed, "now you as well!"

Saul's grip on her wrist slackened slightly. "What?"

"He threatened to kill me if I didn't help him," she sobbed, noticing with appreciation that her nose was already snivelling and her long eyelashes drenched. "What could I do? I was so scared..." She made herself small, like a little girl, and looked up into her father's eyes uncertainly. When he let go of her wrist, she burrowed into him, her arms around his waist, covering herself with his cloak.

"Oh, Michal," said Saul in a thick voice, "Michal, I'm sorry..."

She didn't let go until he was actually patting her head. Then she turned away, wiping her eyes.

Be safe, David, she thought.

But would he be? Would he be fast enough, and strong enough, and clever enough to escape her father?

She had to hope so.

CHAPTER 19

The Company of Prophets

"So you see that's the whole point. That's what it means to be God's people."

The man who'd been speaking sat back against the tree trunk, looking satisfied. The others in the circle nodded thoughtfully. David studied their faces one by one as he let the speaker's words settle in his mind.

They were prophets, all of them: they knew the Lord so well that sometimes he spoke his words through their lips. They lived here together in secluded Naioth, and Samuel had brought David to stay with them. He'd been in their company for several days now: talking and praying and singing and listening...

Nathan, one of the younger members of the circle, had a furrowed brow. "But if that's true," he said, "if we're supposed to be displaying our God to the rest of the world, then how..."

He trailed off.

In a completely different voice, low and tense, he said, "David."

David followed his gaze. They were sitting in a wide open space, fringed by small huts and dotted with shady trees. Opposite was a stone building with an upper floor. The servant who normally sat up there as a lookout was leaning out of his window and waving at them frantically.

David sprang up. "They've come."

Saul had discovered him. It had happened at last.

He felt strangely calm. On light feet he ran to stand beneath the lookout's window.

"Four of them at least," the man told him, "on the road from Ramah. They've ducked out of view now. I guess they think they'll take you by surprise."

"They're armed, presumably?"

"I couldn't see."

They would be, though. Saul's men would take no chances. David was a good fighter and they knew it.

The ground around the lookout building was paved with a few large flat stones. David lifted one of them and felt underneath for the short sword he'd stashed there. His fingers closed with satisfaction around the rough leather sling he'd wound around its handle.

Replacing the stone, he took one look back at Nathan and the other prophets, still sitting quietly beneath their tree. Then he ran out of Naioth.

But they were right there, on the road, making for him.

"David!" shouted their leader, a burly man David recognised as one of Saul's newer attendants. "David, you can't hide!"

It was true. David stood his ground warily. "You've come from Saul?"

"He wants you back in Gibeah," answered the man. "It's the feast in a few days."

"He tried to kill me." David gripped his sword.

"He wants you back now." The man smiled, spreading his hands out to show there were no weapons in them. "Come back with us."

The other three men held daggers, and they were making no move to drop them. David narrowed his eyes. Maoz was the one on the right: a man who beat his servants when he was drunk. David recognised the others as well: one of them took bribes, and the other had tricked a widow last month into buying a half-starved donkey for five times what it was really worth. At various times David had tried to persuade Saul to punish all three of these men, or at the very least to stop employing them. And these were the messengers Saul sent to fetch him?

He stepped backwards. Four of them… If they wanted to overpower him, they could.

The Lord is king, our God is king, he chanted to himself inwardly.

Help me, he added as he took another step back.

Then he heard a thin voice behind him. A *singing* voice.

"The Lord is king, our God is king.
Praise the Lord who rescues,
the Lord who loves his people…"

It was Samuel's voice; he must have come out of his hut. Had he realised that Saul's thugs were here? His voice was reedy but confident and calm. The voices of the other prophets joined in one by one. David trembled. They were a world away from him; they had nothing to do with the danger he was in…

Except perhaps they did.

Maoz and the rest had stopped focusing on David. He saw their expressions change: surprise, then shock, then something else… a kind of crumpling. It happened to them all at once. They fell to their knees; their knives dropped from their hands and clattered to the ground. They lifted their faces, closed their eyes, and started to sing. Just like Samuel and the others.

Prophets behind him, thugs in front of him—and all singing God's praises. David marvelled.

He hadn't expected the Lord to do *that*.

The following day there were more messengers. This time they had friendlier faces.

"Oren," David said, shaking the man's hand in surprise. Oren was a prosperous farmer; he had been a soldier once, Jonathan's armour-bearer too, but he hadn't served Saul's family for years now.

"I come from the king," said Oren, "and from Jonathan. They both thought you would trust me." He bowed formally. "You're welcome back in Gibeah, David. You don't need to be afraid."

"Saul tried to kill me," David told him.

But Oren shrugged. "He gets into rages, doesn't he? Sounds like you know that better than anyone. Jonathan really thinks you're safe."

David shook his head. "You didn't see Saul's face."

Oren shrugged again. "Do you trust Jonathan?"

"Of course, but…"

He trailed off. Oren's face had gone slack. So had his companion's. David wheeled round to see Samuel standing there again, his withered arms raised in prayer.

"The Lord is king," muttered Oren and the other messenger weakly. "A fortress who cannot be moved!" Then they collapsed on the ground.

David took a step back.

A fortress.

The Lord was his fortress.

The Lord had intervened, again.

But did that mean that Oren was his enemy just as much as Maoz and the others? Had God wanted to stop Oren speaking? Had he been lying?

"Is it safe in Gibeah, or not?" David murmured.

How could he possibly know?

David whirled his sling around his head and heard the satisfying thwack as the stone hit the log he'd set up as a target. He picked up another stone and fitted it to his sling, musing.

It would be the new moon feast in a couple of days. Maybe he *should* go. If there was any time to make peace with Saul, it'd be then, when the wine was flowing… Saul wouldn't be able to attack him with so many people around, and maybe once they'd got through the feast everything would be all right again.

The next stone went too far to the left. A bad shot. David pursed his lips, uneasy, trying to concentrate.

Jonathan would know what to do. Had Oren been telling the truth—did Jonathan really think he was safe? If only David could be sure. If only he could see Jonathan himself, without any danger from Saul. If only he could see Michal.

But Jonathan and Michal were both in Gibeah. And so was the king.

David breathed in and out. He bent to pick up another stone. Then a voice called his name.

There was a commotion by the lookout tower. Another messenger? David wrapped his sling around his hand and ran lightly across the clearing.

There was a man crouching on the ground, his hands tearing at his clothes. His sword lay abandoned in the dust; a crumpled cloak too. David picked them up. His thumbs rubbed at the cloak's embroidery; its edge was thick with gold threads. It seemed familiar…

He went cold.

No, he must have made a mistake. This couldn't be Saul's cloak.

That couldn't be Saul.

He came closer, and the small crowd moved out of his way. He knelt down. It *was* Saul. The king stared at him—with anger? Sorrow?

"David," he cried, "David—" But he wasn't in control of himself. Tears were rolling down his cheeks and his jaw shook. David had seen Saul in many moods, but never like this.

He gripped the king's hands, willing strength into him. He leaned forwards and pressed his forehead against Saul's: "Be still, be still."

But Saul flung himself away with a horrible groan. His fingers clawed at the dirt. "Oh Lord, Lord," he raved.

"The Spirit of the Lord is upon him," came Samuel's voice gently. "We should leave him." He looked at David very seriously. "I think the king will be like this for a while."

David nodded. He understood.

It was time to go to Gibeah.

CHAPTER 20

Three Arrows

"Five silver shekels."

"Five! You're out of your mind. Two."

"Four."

"Three."

"Three and a half."

"Done." The trader held out a long-fingered hand. Jonathan shook it. Three and a half shekels for seven sacks of barley flour. Well, it could have been worse.

Jonathan nodded to his servant, who began to load the sacks onto a handcart. He himself walked on. Next stop, Oren's farm. Surely he could get a good deal from Oren, of all people; and his cheeses were the best in the whole of Benjamin. And Jonathan had chosen the sheep to be killed, and they already had a good store of olives and wine and fruit… Yes, it was all coming together. Everyone would be well-fed and happy. It would be a good feast.

He paused, noticing a tall man with a large nose skulking by the town's main gate. Maoz. He was talking to some barefoot boys, giving them each a coin... Jonathan bit his lip. He'd often wished his father would send the man away from Gibeah. What was he up to now?

The boys scuttled away and Maoz watched them greedily. Jonathan watched too, his heart sinking as he saw one of them reach his tiny fingers for an old woman's badly-secured purse.

"Hey—" he said, stepping forward—but was it better to stop the boys themselves or deal with the one who'd paid them? Hesitating, Jonathan glanced back at Maoz—then grunted in frustration as he saw that he'd already melted away.

He was nowhere. Had he gone out of the gate? Jonathan darted out into the road—he'd be sure to catch him if he could see him—but Maoz wasn't there either.

Unless... unless he was in the ditch. There was a deep channel by the side of the road, too deep to see to the bottom from this angle. Jonathan crept towards it, painfully aware of the gravel that might crunch under his sandals and give him away. He moved slowly, slowly, his body tense, ready to pounce—

He looked down into the ditch. Eyes stared back up at him.

He knew those eyes.

"Hello," David said simply.

Jonathan spluttered. "What are you doing *there*?"

"Oh, just relaxing," said David, his face growing mischievous for a moment. "Don't you find that roadside ditches are a good place to spend time?"

Jonathan pulled a face at him, and David became more serious.

"I want to talk to you but without people seeing. I got here sooner than I expected. I thought I'd hide here until nightfall." David's mouth twisted. "I thought it probably wasn't safe to go and find Michal."

Jonathan frowned. "But you don't need to hide. Look, come out of there—"

But David shook his head. "Jonathan. Tell me, what have I done wrong, that your father is trying to kill me?"

Your father. Jonathan rankled at that. *Your father,* as if it was all Jonathan's fault! "You're not going to die," he said crossly. "My father doesn't do anything without letting me know. He swore an oath to me he wouldn't kill you, remember?"

"I'll swear an oath myself if it'll make you believe me. *Saul wants to kill me.* He knows you'll be grieved by it, so he hasn't told you. But I swear—*I swear,*" repeated David, "he really means it this time. As surely as the Lord lives, there is only a step between me and death."

David's cheeks were flushed and his eyes burning.

Jonathan swallowed.

"Whatever you want me to do," he said, "I'll do."

The lichen on the old stone field-marker was pale green with yellow at the edges. It spread out in random furls across the rock. David traced the pattern with his eyes: the big blob there, the bare patch here... He sighed. He'd been staring at this rock for two whole days. Even in his worst imaginings this was not how he'd thought his return to Gibeah would go.

The field was damp too. They should have chosen a better place for him to hide: somewhere higher up, where he could get the fresh air in his nostrils. David could see the hilltops from here, scattered with sheep. He wished he were a shepherd again, and free.

There were eighty-one tiny red flowers within an arm's length of him; he'd counted them five times. He surveyed them again dully. "One, two..." At least counting flowers was better than letting his mind fill up with fear.

He'd got to seventy-three when he heard Jonathan's voice.

At last! David crept closer to the rock, every hair on his body standing on end. If it was bad news, Jonathan wouldn't come close; it'd be too risky to be seen together. He'd send his servant instead. They'd agreed a code. If Jonathan shot three arrows, then David had to flee.

"Run and get the arrows I shoot." Jonathan's voice was distant but audible. David heard the ground crunching as his friend took up a shooting position on the far side of the field. Almost immediately an arrow whizzed past the stone and sank into the ground.

One.

A second arrow shot into the air, landing short this time.

Two.

There was the sound of small feet running through the field: the dull thud of damp earth, the slap of sandals. The boy was coming to fetch the arrows. He was coming closer—

Jonathan shot another arrow, over the boy's head. That made three.

Now David knew. Saul still wanted to kill him.

"Hurry! Go quickly! Don't stop!" called Jonathan, his voice high.

The boy panted as he sped up, thinking the instructions were for him. David shrank back, moving his arm over his face to hide it—but the boy was no danger: he was concentrating on pulling the arrows out of the ground.

One. Two. Three. The third came out of the earth with a soft pop.

When the boy's footsteps had retreated again, David peered cautiously around the stone. Jonathan was giving the boy his bow, pointing towards Gibeah. The child was going... had gone.

David stood up.

As he came near, Jonathan's face was streaked with tears.

"I told him you had gone home to Bethlehem, and that was why you weren't at the feast," he said, "like we agreed. And he said—he said…"

David watched Jonathan's mouth try to shape itself around the words.

"He lost his temper," he suggested.

"He shouted at me," whispered Jonathan hoarsely. "He shouted, *You have sided with the son of Jesse to your shame.*"

A fresh tear burst from Jonathan's eye.

Silently and slowly, keeping his gaze on his friend's face, David knelt to the ground. He bowed forward, stretching himself out in the dirt. Then he did the same thing twice more.

It was the best thing he could think of to do.

"They bowed to my father just like that," Jonathan said tearfully, "when he first became king."

Then as David got up, Jonathan added fiercely, "I won't be king. That's what my father said, and he's right. You will be king, not me."

I don't see how, thought David, but Jonathan was stepping forward, nose to nose with David, fists balled by his sides. "Swear to me," Jonathan said, "swear it again, that you will always be kind to me and to my family."

David nodded. "The Lord is witness between you and me," he said slowly, "and between my descendants and your descendants for ever."

Then they clasped hands one last time.

It was dangerous to stay together. But it was too hard not to. David found that tears were now coursing down his own cheeks: he wrapped his arms around Jonathan and allowed himself to weep freely.

"Go in peace," said Jonathan eventually, stepping back.

David knew what he meant: *You're not my enemy, and I'm not yours. I won't fight against you. I won't stand in your way.*

But Saul *was* David's enemy, and David had to flee.

He let go of Jonathan's hand and paced away across the mud.

PART FIVE

The Wilderness

Seven years later

CHAPTER 21

The Chase

The water was sparkling, cool, delicious. David held the skin-bottle high in the air and let every last drop glug out of it into his parched mouth.

"Aaaaah," he sighed in satisfaction. "Thanks be to the Lord, who gives us such a thing as water." He jumped up in pleasure, feeling the energy coursing back into his veins. "Thanks be to the Lord, who is *better* than water!"

"And thanks be to Joab, who went to fetch the water," said Abishai.

David grinned. "Oh yes indeed," he said, cuffing his companion lightly round the head, "and thanks be, I don't doubt, to Joab's poor old brother, who sent him instead of going himself?"

Abishai's beard twitched. "It was hot."

"It's always hot," said David. He bent to stretch out his tired limbs, then straightened up. "Come on, then, let's go back."

He slung the rock-rabbit over his shoulder as the two of them trudged away. That was all they had managed to kill after a whole day of hunting: one little rock-rabbit. Abishai had had a shot at a raven circling high above, but his arrow had fallen short. David smiled: at least the rock-rabbit wasn't going to be heavy to carry back to camp. And tomorrow would be another day. They might catch a whole gazelle tomorrow. One each, even.

Gradually the camp appeared in front of them. Well, they called it a camp, but that was stretching it. A spread-out collection of rugged tents was what it was, and it changed every day: a tent added here, another gone there, so that the whole encampment rippled unpredictably across the desert like some huge restless animal. They'd been up in the mountains not long ago, but now they'd come further east. It was wise to keep moving.

"Chief," said one of the lookouts in greeting as David and Abishai reached the first of the low grey tents. "Good hunting?"

"Not so good," answered David.

"The Lord will provide."

"That's true: he always has."

It was good to keep remembering it; good to have men to tell it to. There were six hundred or so of them now, David's men, plus their wives and children: a little kingdom of misfits and nomads. They even had a priest among them—Abiathar, who had run from Saul, taking only the ephod and the Urim and Thummim, and had been among the first to join David. They all billowed through the wilderness together, like their ancestors whom God had led out of Egypt. Trying to be God's people. Trying to find enough to eat.

"Chief." Ahimelek's voice this time, sounding urgent as he unfolded his thin limbs from a cushion outside his tent. "The scouts you sent up the mountain. They're back."

David exchanged glances with Abishai. "Saul's there?"

"He's camped just the other side of the mountain. On the northern tip, near that ravine."

David nodded. "How many men?"

"Three thousand, maybe. He's picked the best warriors, the scouts said."

Ahimelek looked worried. He always did. He'd been a wanderer most of his life and he knew the dangers of the desert better than anyone.

But David knew Saul.

He unslung the rock-rabbit from his shoulders and dumped it on the ground. "First of all I want to eat," he announced. "But after that—who will go down to Saul's camp with me?"

Ahimelek's narrow eyebrows furrowed. But Abishai clapped David on the shoulder eagerly. "I'll go."

They climbed the mountain fast: it was easier going in the dark, now that the sun had stopped glaring. They paused once or twice when they heard a noise, fearing lions or wolves; but whatever it was that had come close, it left them alone.

"Probably just a badger," whispered Abishai, scratching his beard.

David liked that about Abishai: he wasn't afraid. He'd been like that right from the start. Abishai had been among the first to come out to the caves in the western desert to find David, soon after he'd run from Gibeah. He'd come with his two brothers, Joab and Asahel: three young men with identical black beards, all of them fierce and ready to follow David wherever he went. They were his nephews, his sister Zeruiah's boys, although they were barely any younger than him.

David had told them he could offer them no real future, but Abishai had retorted that there was no future for them under the rule of Saul, either. So the sons of Zeruiah had stayed.

They reached the top of the mountain. The sky loomed huge and dark, like a gigantic tent put up by God to shelter them. Ahead, downhill, lay Saul's men.

David swallowed. Maybe this would be the last time. Maybe Saul would finally give up the chase and leave him in peace.

The king had obviously travelled fast and light: he'd known David wouldn't be in the same spot for long. He and his soldiers had brought no tents, just stretched themselves out on the ground to sleep. *The sky shelters them,* David thought, *just as much as it does us.*

Spears were stuck in the dry earth all around the soldiers, but they had no more protection than that: even the lookout was snoring at his post. Had the Lord made them sleep? David and Abishai moved closer, warily pacing around the slumbering army. They both spotted Saul at the same time: his gold-edged robe glinted. David recognised Abner's bulky shape nearby. Between the two cousins sat a round water jug.

David shivered. Saul was only fifty paces away. A spear-throw would be all it would take. One quick movement, and no more Saul. No more being chased through the wilderness. No more wandering. One quick movement and David could go home.

He thought of Michal. Saul had made her marry some other man, he'd heard; she had a different life now. She probably never thought of him.

His eyes narrowed. Saul had taken so much! And with one movement, one spear-throw, it could all be over…

Abishai's hand gripped David's arm. He'd had the same thought. "God has delivered your enemy into your hands!" he whispered excitedly. "Let me do it—let me pin him to the ground. One thrust of the spear. I won't strike him twice. I won't need to."

"No." There could be no other answer: David knew it really. He found Abishai's hand and squeezed it back. "Don't destroy him. Who can lay a hand on the Lord's anointed?"

"But chief, after all this time—now's your *chance*—"

Abishai had spoken too loudly. Close to David's feet, one of the soldiers stirred. David and Abishai froze, hearts thudding.

The man turned over, gave a little moan, and settled down again.

David looked at his nephew. "As surely as the Lord lives," he whispered carefully, "one day the Lord himself will strike Saul, or his time will come and he'll die, or he'll go into battle and perish that way. But the Lord forbid that I should lay a hand on the Lord's anointed."

There was silence. Sulkily, Abishai said, "Then why are we here?"

David smiled. "Get his spear and that jug," he told him, "and let's go."

Together they tiptoed through the mass of sleeping soldiers. Abishai pulled Saul's spear out of the ground and David picked up the water jug. As he bent down he looked into Saul's face. It was deeply lined, the beard streaked with grey: he seemed to have grown decades older in the space of only a few years. David found himself feeling sorry for him.

They danced away into the darkness, light-hearted and triumphant; but not up and over the mountain again. David led Abishai downhill, down to the narrow ravine and up the steep cliff on the other side. He had to strap Saul's deep-bellied jug to his back to leave his hands free for climbing.

"Here goes," David said when they got to the top.

Then he started to yell. "Abner! ABNER!"

They could see nothing in the darkness, but they heard movement across the ravine.

"Abner!" David called again. "Aren't you going to answer me?"

Muffled voices roused themselves from sleep; the commander hissed at them to stay silent. There was a pause. Then, warily, Abner called out. "Who are you?"

David grinned to Abishai. He cupped his hands around his mouth to call again. "Why didn't you guard your lord the king? Someone came to destroy him. You did not guard your master, the Lord's anointed."

He could just imagine Abner's horror. He heard brief, frantic movement in the camp. He cried out again: "Yes, look around you. Where's the king's spear? Where's the jug that was near his head?"

More frantic rustling. Then a new voice trembled in the darkness. Saul's.

"Is that your voice, David my son?"

My son. David closed his eyes for a moment. "Yes it is, my lord the king," he shouted. "Why is my lord pursuing his servant? What have I done?"

The ravine was silent.

"If the Lord has sent you against me, may he accept an offering, a sacrifice, and stop being angry with me," David called. "If it's some adviser that's persuaded you to get rid of me—let them be cursed!" His hands were trembling; he curled them into fists. "They have driven me away—told me to go and serve other gods—want me to leave the kingdom of the God of Israel. But Saul—" and David could not keep the sob out of his voice as he spoke the king's name—"do not let my blood fall to the ground far from the presence of the Lord!"

I don't need to come home, he added silently. *Just let me be at peace in the wilderness. Just let me stay in Israel. In God's land.*

His words seemed to bounce off the rocks, the echo fading into silence. On the opposite hillside a flame flickered into life, casting its small light across the valley. But it was still impossible to see Saul's face.

At last his voice came back again. "I have sinned. Come back, David, my son. You considered my life precious—I will not harm you again."

David blinked.

"I have been terribly wrong," added Saul. His voice shook.

David found that he was shaking too.

CHAPTER 22

Out of Israel

B ut it was too good to be true.

"I knew it," said Abishai. "Maybe he meant it at the time, David, but it was never going to last. Saul doesn't keep his word."

"Someone must have talked him out of it," added his brother Joab, more quietly. "Abner, maybe." He fingered the blade of his axe.

David said nothing. Instead he gathered his reins and slapped his horse on the shoulder. "Yah!" He shot forward, ahead of the others. He didn't want to talk right now.

Saul's men had come after them yet again. Now David was leading his straggle of followers out of Israel. What choice did he have? If he stayed, Saul was not going to let him live. Eventually he'd catch him. David *had* to leave.

So they were going to Gath. David had had a bitter taste in his mouth ever since he'd made the decision.

Now, as he got within reach of the city and reined his horse in, he wished he could vomit.

Gath was where Goliath had come from. Gath was a Philistine city.

They were going to beg their worst enemies for help.

David spat on the ground, then twisted his mouth and began to pray silently instead.

When the men caught up, David made most of them wait in a big mass outside the city. He took Abishai and Joab with him into Gath: his surest fighters. The three of them rode in on horseback like kings, keeping their faces proud and imperious. They demanded an audience with the ruler of the city. They got one.

He was sitting in a room built of stone, one elbow propped on an arm of his golden chair. Achish. The king of Gath had a narrow face with arched eyebrows. "David," he said, arching one of them even further.

David met his gaze.

If he was going to have to live among the Philistines, he was going to do it on his own terms.

He bowed, but not deeply. "I have six hundred men," he told the king in a careless tone, "waiting outside the city. Hardened men, used to fighting. We will pledge our swords to you, if you choose."

As Achish looked him up and down, David remembered Saul doing the same thing, years ago in the valley of Elah before he'd killed Goliath. *Who will remove this disgrace from Israel?* his younger self had asked. His own remembered words seemed to accuse him now. He was going over to the enemy. Serving those who hated the Lord.

But I love the Lord, he told himself. *Is that enough?*

When he'd fought Goliath he'd known so clearly what the right thing to do was. But now… Now everything seemed unbearably complicated.

Achish's gaze had returned to David's face. "*David has killed his tens of thousands*—that's how the song used to go, is it not?" He stood up, walking away around the room: his robe swished about his ankles. "David, killer of thousands of Philistines."

David kept his feet planted on the floor, betraying no nervousness. Joab and Abishai remained silent behind him.

"David, *king of Israel,* they even said," the king continued. His head snapped round back to David again suddenly. "And look at you now."

He wants to humiliate me. Oh, well, David could cope with that. He relaxed his stance, smiling easily, one hand on his sword hilt.

Achish scowled. "You come to me asking for quarter."

"We come to you offering our services," replied David smoothly. "And, yes, we will need a place to stay."

"How do I know you are not spies?"

David laughed. "Does a loyal servant of Saul spend

years on the run from him?"

Achish considered this. "No." He looked away again, resuming his slow swish around the room. "Six hundred fighters."

It seemed to be a question. "Yes," David told him, "and each worth three ordinary men." He paused. "Men with a reputation for fair dealing, I might add."

Achish nodded; this was not news to him, David could see. David's men had dealt with many a bandit or robber over the years, protected travellers and widows, helped solve arguments in the villages they'd passed through. They'd made the country safe. It showed people what God was like.

"All right." Achish offered his hand to David to shake. "You can let your men camp in Gath. But I want them divided up—ten at the most in any settlement. And they go where I tell them."

David smiled pleasantly. He did not shake Achish's hand.

The king scowled again. "Well?"

"If I have found favour in your eyes," said David, still smiling, "let a place be assigned to me in one of the country towns. I and my men will live there." *And I'll be in charge of them,* he added silently.

Achish's eyebrows rose.

"My men are waiting outside the city as we speak," David said. "Armed."

There was silence.

Then Achish held out his hand again.

"You can have Ziklag," he said. "East of here. But every week, you report to me."

David grasped the king's hand. He hadn't expected him to be beaten so quickly.

"Our swords are your swords," he said.

Please, he added silently in prayer, *please, Lord, please forgive me.*

He did not like Ziklag.

Everyone else seemed ecstatic: "A whole town of our own!" "You got Achish right where you wanted him!" But David was homesick for the rough deserts and dank caves of Israel.

"At least we were in the right kingdom," he muttered as he rode back through Ziklag's ramshackle gates one evening after making his third report to Achish in Gath. The king had been bad-tempered, accusing David of taking his money and his lands and doing nothing with them.

"Make raids!" he'd cried, his eyebrows hunched. "Fight! Win something! Do you think I can't throw you out?"

David had had to promise three attacks on non-Philistine villages in the next three weeks. It was obvious what Achish wanted—obvious why Ziklag had been the town he'd chosen for David and his men. David had been a fool not to see it: Ziklag was right in the east. Close to Israelite land.

Achish wanted David to attack his own people.

He sat back in his saddle, looking around at Ziklag's untidy streets as he passed through them. Men and women bowed to him, looking frightened. David frowned.

"Who can we fight?" he cried when he reached his house. "Who should we attack?"

Joab and the others stepped back. David snorted in irritation. He was normally even-tempered; they were surprised by his anger. But he was right to be angry! This situation was impossible!

He glared at his companions. "Well?"

Just then footsteps came into the house behind him: soft footprints, hesitant ones.

He whirled around. Two children stood in the doorway, a girl and her little brother. They were ragged and barefoot and their eyes were very large.

"Tell him, go on." A woman had followed them in—no, she'd ushered them forwards. "He won't bite," she said, winking at David.

He felt his cheeks go red as all the jaggedness went out of his anger. He crouched down and spoke gently. "What is it?"

But the children just stared at him, silent.

"They're orphans. Their family's farm has just been destroyed," the woman told him. "By Amalekites."

"Amalekites!"

"Our armies almost destroyed the Amalekites years ago," Joab said behind David. "Saul had the chance. The Lord told him to destroy them, I heard. But he didn't quite do it."

David nodded. He stood up.

"It sounds like we have someone to fight."

CHAPTER 23

Burning

So that was how they lived. For a year and four months they stayed in Ziklag. They raided the Amalekites and the Geshurites and others, steering clear of Israelite land; then David spun elaborate stories for Achish about how they'd attacked this village or that farm in the region of Judah. His own tribe! But Achish believed him.

They rebuilt Ziklag's gates and made the farms around it safe. They built an altar and made sacrifices to the Lord. Ziklag became David's own little kingdom—until the day the news came that the Philistine rulers had all met together and agreed to gather their forces once again. A proper war. Their target? David knew it before he'd even been told: knew it by the way his stomach turned and his heart quickened as Achish looked him up and down.

Israel.

"You must understand," Achish told him, "that you and your men will accompany me in the army."

David swallowed. He bowed low so that Achish wouldn't see his face. He kept his eyes on the ground.

"Then," he said calmly, "you will see for yourself what your servant can do."

They marched up the coast and then inland; the Israelites scattered before them. It was going to be just as bad as the previous great war, when the Philistines had taken over most of Benjamin, and Saul had barely clung to Gibeah. Worse than that, even. The cities of Ephraim had fallen and half of Manasseh too. Every time the scouts came back they laughed in triumph: "Retreating again! Does Saul call himself a king?"

David stayed silent.

But the other captains didn't trust him.

"Hear that, Hebrew?" one called out mockingly after the latest spies had made their report. "That's all your old friends, isn't it? Cowards, the lot of them."

Achish rose and hit the man around the head, hard. "David is one of ours," he said gruffly.

"Well, they all will be soon," said the man sulkily, shrinking away. "Won't have a choice once we've conquered them all."

David thought of Jonathan. He'd be out there in the mountains with Saul right now… He'd die rather than be ruled by the Philistines. So would Michal.

David felt his limbs start to shake and he ducked

away out of Achish's tent, feeling sick.

Where did I go wrong? What can I do? He was back in Israel, but Israel seemed doomed—and David would be part of the destruction.

Should I have killed Saul? he asked himself, *made myself king?* He'd be a better ruler than Saul, he knew that.

But Saul was the Lord's anointed.

As for David's anointing, all those years ago… and as for Jonathan's certainty that he would be king… He shook his head bitterly. Maybe Samuel *had* made a mistake after all.

He saw two of the Philistine rulers coming towards him, surrounded by a buzz of attendants. They were dressed for battle already: armour encased their bodies and heavy swords swung at their sides. They glared at him as he passed. He bowed low, right to the ground— that was what you were supposed to do as soon as you saw them. He stayed there until their footsteps had gone away. Then he wiped his forehead and straightened up.

There was a song he'd sung once, long ago.

"The Lord is righteous,
he loves justice,
the upright will see his face."

But what if I'm not upright anymore? he asked God silently.

"David."

He'd barely made it back to his own tent when he heard Achish hurrying towards him. The king put his hand on David's shoulder, forestalling his bow. His face looked troubled.

"David," he sighed, "as surely as your God lives, you have been reliable. I have found no fault in you."

There was a "but" coming. David's heart thumped with anticipation.

Achish sighed again. "But the other rulers don't approve of you. They think you'll turn tail and fight on the side of Saul." His hand gripped David's shoulder hard. "*Don't* do anything to displease them. Turn back and go home. Go in peace."

David gaped. "But what—why can't I go and fight?"

Achish shook his head sadly. "The commanders have said, *He must not go up with us into battle.* Their word is final. But you are free to go. Get up early and leave in the morning, as soon as it's light."

David made himself nod his head. "Yes, sir," he said.

Not everyone was pleased.

"We wanted to fight," grumbled Abishai, again, on the third day of travelling back towards Ziklag.

David sighed. "Against Israel?"

"Against *Saul.* Come on, it would have been good to see him got rid of at last."

David shook his head, uneasy. "Well, we're not going to."

"This way, we stay safe," Ahimelek pointed out. "And we'll be in a good position once the war is over. When the dust settles we can make a plan."

"What kind of plan?"

"Well, to make you king, maybe."

David didn't answer that.

"And aren't you looking forward to seeing your wife again, Abishai?" added Ahimelek lightly.

Everyone knew Abishai and his wife did not get along. He scowled into his beard, and dug his spurs into his horse.

They'd hardly seen a soul as they'd come back south, except occasional Israelite shepherds who ran away when they saw them coming. "Don't leave your sheep!" David wanted to roar at them, but how were they to know David wasn't a Philistine?

It was his own men he really needed to worry about: he knew that. It wasn't just Abishai who was grumbling. Last night Joab had pulled David away from the fire to give him news of more discontentment.

"Some of the men are angry," he had said, "that they had to go all that way, leave their wives and children, all for nothing."

David groaned. "But how could I—"

"I know," agreed Joab, "you couldn't have predicted being sent away. But they'll be all right once they see their families again." His voice dropped conspiratorially. "Those aren't the ones you need to worry about."

David frowned. "Go on."

"Some of the men are saying you've got no plan. They had thought you wanted to kill Saul and then fight the Philistines. Or get the Philistines to make you the king of Israel, maybe. I don't know. Anyway, the point is, they're asking what's next. Are we really just going to go back to Ziklag and be good boys? Some of them think we shouldn't even be here—we should be fighting for Israel. Some of them think you should be trying to get more power among the Philistines."

David swallowed. "I've never wanted to fight against Saul," he said. "He's God's chosen king. I've just—look, I haven't made plans, I just wanted to survive, and worship the Lord—it's not up to me, it's up to him—"

"And he has got you into a bit of a mess," answered Joab softly.

They looked at each other.

"I'm just telling you," said Joab with a shrug. "I don't want a bust-up. So I'm telling you. You need to give the men confidence again."

David nodded slowly. He could see his friend was right.

Still, he was going to do things his way.

"When we get back to Ziklag," he said, "I'll consult the priest. He can ask the Lord what we should do. Let's just get home first."

Joab squeezed his arm. "You know best."

Now they were nearly there, and apart from Abishai's complaints David had heard no stirring among the men. He'd been right: home was in their eyes. Only one more hill, just one more climb and then they'd see it. Then they'd see...

A plume of smoke.

David smelled it as soon as he spotted it: the bitter scent of burning, choking the clean air.

Hearth fires didn't make a cloud that big.

They came over the ridge. David was numb; the shouts of horror around him barely registered as he stared down the hill.

Ziklag was burning.

CHAPTER 24

No Time to Lose

"Let's kill him."

"Let's KILL HIM!"

The men had stones in their fists and murder in their eyes. David was strong but they were too. They didn't want him anymore—they were too angry—everything was going to end—he was going to die, just like the women and children they'd left behind, left behind to be burned—

"STOP!"

It was Abiathar. The priest. He'd staggered up from Ziklag, ashen-faced, weeping, and flung his arms out as if his body could stop the stoning.

"Abiathar."

"You escaped?"

"Who was it? Who burned Ziklag?"

The men were lowering their fists; David breathed in and out. He grabbed Abiathar and repeated the men's questions. "Who was it? Who did it?"

"It was the Amalekites," sobbed Abiathar, his hand gripping onto David's clothes. "They came at dawn. I was on the hill—they didn't see me—but they took everything. Everyone."

"They took them?" David grasped at this. "They didn't kill them?"

"No. They'll sell them as slaves probably—"

"No, they won't." David stood up as tall as he could and glared at the crowd of men. "Listen to me. I'm grieving too. I have no strength—I have no strength left to weep, just like you."

He took in their faces. Their eyes were livid, but they were listening.

"But we can find strength in the Lord." Quickly David turned to Abiathar. "Bring the ephod. We'll ask God what to do."

He said nothing while Abiathar scrambled away; just prayed, desperately, that the Lord would keep the men's hands by their sides. One or two had already dropped their rocks; the rage was leaking out of them as grief took over again.

But he would need their rage. As soon as Abiathar returned, David asked his question. "Shall I pursue the Amalekites?"

Abiathar pulled the stones out of the linen pouch, showed them to David. Yes, the markings read.

"We will succeed in the rescue," David announced,

glaring around at the men again. "There's no time to lose." He sprinted away, grabbed the sword that he'd left hanging by his horse's flank, and held it high in the air. "Who's with me?" he roared at the crowd of men.

"YAAAAAAHH!" came the response.

They snatched up their stones again. But this time they weren't aiming at David.

They lost a third of the men on the way; after so much travelling they were too exhausted and fell behind. David didn't care. "It doesn't matter how many of us there are!" he urged the rest. "The Lord will give the Amalekites into our hands! Go! Go!"

In one of the last fields before the desert they found an Egyptian, a dark-skinned boy with cropped black hair. He was curled up in the dust, begging for water.

"Shall we kill him?" said someone eagerly.

"He's half dead already," observed someone else.

But David reached for his skin of water. "Let's see if we can revive him."

He had a cake of closely–packed raisins somewhere; he found it and began to break it up, offering the boy the sweet dried fruit one at a time.

The boy opened his dry lips to take the food. He coughed, but then chewed and swallowed. David stared into his face eagerly, watching his eyes become gradually brighter.

"Who do you belong to?" he asked the boy once he was able to sit up on his own.

"I'm the slave of an Amalekite," answered the Egyptian slowly. His tongue was still thick with thirst, and he squeezed another drop of water onto it as David patted his back encouragingly. "My master abandoned me when I became ill three days ago," he went on in a dazed voice. "We were returning from raiding… We raided some territory belonging to Judah. And we burned Ziklag."

The men around them suddenly loomed, clenching their fists. David waved them back.

"Could you lead me down to this raiding party?" he asked the boy gently. "Do you know which way they went?"

The boy looked frightened. "Swear—swear to me, before God," he stuttered, "that you won't kill me, or—or hand me over to my master. Swear it. Then I'll take you to them."

"I swear it," declared David at once, with a fierce glance at his men.

They shuffled back, looking at their toes.

David allowed himself a small smile.

They were all on foot, but in the next village they found a donkey for the boy to sit on. He pointed the way, still clutching his cake of raisins. The land was flat here and trackless; soil had given way to sand. They were in Amalekite territory now, and further south than most of them had ever been.

"There." At last the boy's voice had a note of triumph in it. David followed his trembling finger as it pointed towards the edge of the dunes. "There."

There: a collection of stunted trees around what looked like a dusty well. Dark figures dotted the trees' shade. Some were clumped together in groups, not moving: tied up, David assumed. Others sprawled gleefully. Their laughter echoed through the dunes.

"There," whispered David, letting go of the donkey's lead rope. "There." He drew his sword.

They fought through the night and well into the following day. The Amalekites were vicious fighters, but an attack seemed to have been the last thing they were expecting: they'd thought all the warriors of both Philistia and Judah had gone up north to the war. So the Amalekites had been scattered widely across the dunes, nowhere near ready to fight, just enjoying the plunder they'd taken.

And what plunder! Picking through the burnt-out fires and collapsed tents after the battle was over, David found whole carts full of wine and huge piles of sacks bursting with grain. Sheep and oxen were tied together in their hundreds, and here and there in the sand was a jewelled casket lying on its side, the golden contents spilling out to gleam and glitter like curious eyes.

This much plunder must have come from a lot of different places: the Amalekites had raided widely and effectively. But the captives were all from Ziklag; and every one of them was there. Not the tiniest child was missing.

David gave Joab a grim smile. "Not such a mess as you thought. Does this restore the men's confidence, do you think?"

Joab bowed his head.

"When we get back to Ziklag," David went on, "I'm sending you to Judah. Go to the elders of the tribe and tell them I'm giving them a portion of the plunder. A lot of it comes from them anyway, and they'll need it if they're to survive the war with the Philistines."

Joab raised his eyebrows. "Then you're supporting Israel?"

"I'm supporting my own tribe," David began, but Abiathar the priest interrupted.

"A wise idea. You'll need the elders of Judah on your side."

"On my—"

Abiathar touched David's arm, much in the way someone would pat a child who was slow at his lessons. "Did I ever tell you what my father told me about Saul's war with the Amalekites, years ago? You know he was a priest too; he travelled with Saul."

"I know. No, you didn't tell me."

"Saul disobeyed God. He was greedy about the plunder... I won't go into all the details. But he disobeyed. And Samuel was angry. Very angry." Abiathar's voice was grave and slow. "My father told me he said to Saul that God was taking the kingdom away from him—tearing it away, like something Saul was clinging onto too hard. God said he'd give the kingdom to one of Saul's neighbours. Someone better than Saul. And it wasn't the first time he'd said it, either."

Gradually, David took in the priest's words. God had already said he was taking the kingdom from Saul? Back when Saul had fought the Amalekites? "That was years ago," he said slowly.

He'd been a child then. He'd been… how old?

David's blood ran cold as he worked it out.

That battle against the Amalekites had happened in the same year Samuel had come to Bethlehem.

The prophet had told Saul he was no longer God's chosen king, and then straight away he had come and anointed David.

That could only mean…

"It was after that," Abiathar went on, "that Saul started to have those mad rages. Then you came. And you killed Goliath, and went on about honouring God, and sang songs about him…"

Quietly, David said, "So that's why he hated me. He thought…"

"He thought you were the one God had chosen."

He didn't just think I was a threat because I won lots of battles and everyone liked me, David realised. *He thought God had actually chosen me as—as Saul's replacement.*

Abiathar said, "And you are, aren't you? God's chosen king?"

David stared at him.

Crowds flowed past them, the women and children of Ziklag chattering as they took their first steps back towards home. They bobbed curtseys to him as they passed, touching his arm gently as if they thought it would bring blessing. But David barely noticed.

"I need to think about all of this," he said at last. "Let's go back to Ziklag. Send the plunder to Judah, as I said."

And find out the news from the north, he added silently. But at the thought of *that,* he felt as if his whole body had turned grey.

CHAPTER 25

The Man Who Killed the King

The messenger came three days after they'd reached Ziklag. David gave instructions to let the travel-worn man wash and eat before he delivered his news, but it was plain already what it would be. The messenger's clothes had been deliberately torn and he had smeared dust and ashes into his forehead and hair. It meant grief.

The Israelites had lost.

David sat waiting numbly for the messenger to reappear. There were others waiting with him, but he didn't meet their eyes. He took up his lyre and strummed it half-heartedly, trying to distract himself. Then he tossed it aside. He stood up, walked two paces, then returned to his chair and sat down again. He could feel a deep groan forming inside himself, but he stayed silent. If he let it out, it would mean acknowledging the start of a new world. A world of sorrow. A world in which—

"My lord." The messenger had stepped into the small room. He flung himself down on the ground, hands outstretched towards David; his fingernails were black with dirt. A bag was still slung around his shoulders.

"Where have you come from?" asked David quietly.

"I have escaped from the Israelite camp," the man said.

"What happened? Tell me."

The man lifted his head. "The men of Israel gathered in the mountains of Gilboa," he said. "We met the Philistines. But they were too strong… The men fled from the battle. Many of them fell and died."

David could imagine it easily: the panic, the confusion. Men tripping over each other to escape, none of them knowing where to go, while their attackers charged after them in red-blooded triumph. He had seen it himself many times. But he'd always been the one attacking.

He swallowed. So, the battle was lost. Israel was lost.

"And Saul and his son Jonathan are dead," the messenger added.

In David's belly, the dark groan deepened.

He stood up. Carefully, he said, "How do you know that Saul and his son Jonathan are dead?"

"I was on Mount Gilboa during the retreat," the man answered eagerly. "Saul and Jonathan were together. They fought off a group of attackers, but more were coming. Jonathan had been wounded. He tried to stagger on but it was too serious. He fell."

David pressed his lips together and blinked back the prickling tears. He had to hear the man out.

"Then there was just Saul, leaning on his spear, with the chariots and their drivers in hot pursuit. He was wounded too. When he turned around and saw me, he called out to me, and I said, What can I do?"

The man was speaking quickly and evenly, as if that would make his story easier to hear. "He asked me who I was," he went on. "I said, an Amalekite."

His eyes flicked up to meet David's for a moment, then snapped back to the floor. *An Amalekite,* thought David. So. Had he been fighting on the side of Israel, or the Philistines?

"Then he said to me, Stand here by me and kill me," the man said flatly. "He said he was in the throes of death already. So I stood beside him and I killed him."

Again his eyes flicked up to David's; this time there was a gleam in them. "The chariots were coming; I knew that after he had fallen, he could not survive."

There was silence. Swiftly, the man pulled at the strap over his shoulders and offered David his leather bag. There was a glint of gold inside. "I took the crown that was on his head and the band on his arm and have brought them here to my lord."

David felt a dim disgust as he saw that the man had come here not in grief but in the hopes of a reward. He'd killed the king of Israel—he'd killed God's chosen king of Israel—and he thought David would be pleased! He should *die,* this man—he'd killed God's anointed king— he should be punished!

The black groan in David's belly at last forced its way up through his throat and out of his mouth, swamping his disgust and rage. He twisted away and hid his face. Saul was dead—Saul, who had once called David his son. And so many men had been lost. And Israel, the nation of Israel, the land the Lord loved. And Jonathan— Jonathan. *Jonathan.*

David seized his tunic in his two hands and wrenched the fabric apart. The hole hung loose and jagged. He wished he could tear his body too: tear it up and destroy it so that he, and not they, had died.

At last he stood again and hung his head. "The mighty have fallen," he said. His voice sounded as bitter as the desert.

There were things to be done. David knew that.

Each day he received more messengers, each with news from a different part of Israel. Dully, he heard of loss after loss. The Israelites had fled—not just the army, the ordinary villagers too—and the Philistines had gleefully moved into their homes, farming their crops, taking their herds and flocks for their own.

The tribe of Judah remained free. It sounded like some parts of the north did too, and the far east across the river. There were rumours that some of Saul's commanders had survived—perhaps even Ishvi, Jonathan's younger brother. But none of it was certain.

David needed to make preparations. Achish and the other Philistine rulers were still celebrating the victory up north, but they would come back before long. Meanwhile the elders of Judah had sent word to say that they had received the plunder from the Amalekites, and were ready to receive David himself.

But David wasn't ready to go to Judah.

He listened to every message carefully, and thanked each messenger. Then he took his lyre and wandered away. He walked for miles through the half-abandoned countryside, and the farmers and shepherds stared at him as if he were mad.

At last he wrote down the words that were in his head.

Saul and Jonathan, the song went,
swifter than eagles,
stronger than lions.
Daughters of Israel, weep for Saul,
who clothed you in scarlet and finery,
who adorned your garments with gold.
How the mighty have fallen in battle!
Jonathan lies slain on the heights.
I grieve for you, Jonathan my brother.
How the mighty have fallen!
The weapons of war have perished!

He sang it to Joab and Abishai and Ahimelek and all the others. They listened gravely. He told them it was to be taught to everyone in his kingdom. No one was ever to forget it.

Then he said to Abiathar, the priest, "Get out the ephod."

He received from God the answer he expected. He was to go up to Judah. They would make him king there— king of the last remaining scrap of Israel. Of the rest too, one day, if they could drive out the Philistines. David was God's anointed.

"All right," he said, as Abiathar dropped the tokens back inside the golden ephod. He stepped back, and clapped Joab and Abishai on the shoulder. "Let's go."

PART SIX

The Kingdom of God

Seven years later

CHAPTER 26

In the East

The room was small but clean: Michal had swept it herself, hours ago, longing for something to keep her hands busy. There was a small clay lamp filled with oil. Occasionally she got up and refilled it. A larger one would have been more sensible—the oil would have run out less quickly—but at least this way there was something to punctuate the hours. She'd refilled it five times so far.

Nights in Mahanaim were always dark. Even when she wasn't staying awake deliberately, Michal often lay with her eyes open, seeing nothing, thinking of the night she had first come here, seven years ago.

"Mahanaim," her father had said, "you'll be safe in Mahanaim, even if the Philistines win." So while he and Jonathan went up to Gilboa to face the enemy, Michal had gone the opposite way. She'd been bundled across the river as the sun set and reached the town after dark. Mahanaim was meant to be a refuge, but it had felt strange and unsafe. Her lamp had run out of oil in the unfamiliar streets, and she'd cried out in shock and fear. Fortunately only Noa, who'd come as her servant, had heard her.

It had been dark when her brother Ishvi had arrived, too, and the others who'd escaped the battle. That time Michal had set plenty of lamps burning, but they had only made the shadows worse. And they had lit up the white eyes which stared out of the men's gaunt and dirty faces. None of them would tell her what had happened. Ishvi just stammered like a child, and then shook in his sleep.

It was Paltiel who told her in the end. Her husband, the one Saul had given her to after David had left. Paltiel knelt at Michal's feet and told her that he hadn't been able to save them, Saul and Jonathan—he'd been too far away…

That had been the darkest moment of all.

Now, seven years later, it was dark again, and the flame of the oil lamp danced thinly in the still room.

Ishvi was chewing his lip. *You're a grown man,* Michal wanted to snap at him, *why not act like it?* But she knew it wouldn't be any use. If he were acting like a grown man—like a king, which was what he was supposed to be—he'd have gone to the battle himself.

A king. Michal felt like spitting. Ishvi was supposed to be the king of Israel; he and Abner had got the territory back from the Philistines. But the Philistines were still in charge really: Ishvi sent them money every year. If he were a proper king, he wouldn't put up with it. He'd be fighting against them.

Instead of which, he was fighting David, who was king of Judah now. Or rather, Abner was fighting in Ishvi's place.

The flame between Michal and her brother guttered: it would need fresh oil again soon. How much longer did they have to wait? Where was Abner?

"It's a long journey," said Ishvi in a wobbly voice. "If they went all the way down to Judah itself, it'll take them a long time to get back."

"If they ever do get back." In her mind Michal added, *I hope Abner doesn't.*

"They will," quivered Ishvi. "Abner is the best war captain in Israel. And Paltiel and the others are good fighters. If anyone can defeat David—"

Michal interrupted him. "I don't know why you want to defeat David anyway," she cut in savagely. "Why not leave him alone? At least *his* kingdom is *free.*"

"*We're* free," he answered, sounding wounded.

But it wasn't true. Israel might have cobbled itself back together but it was like an old leather bag full of holes. And all the wealth that leaked out went to the enemy.

Whereas Judah and David were free. Properly, fully free. Michal couldn't help wondering what it was like. What *he* was like, all these years later.

"Abner says—" began Ishvi, but Michal interrupted him again.

"Oh, *Abner* says. When will you stop listening to him and be your own man?"

Ishvi's pasty face wobbled. "He's the best cap—"

"Our father listened to him for years," Michal went on, ignoring him. "I'm sure it was Abner who persuaded him to get rid of David. Most foolish thing Saul ever did. And he did a lot of foolish things."

"It wasn't—"

"He chased his best fighter into exile, Ishvi," she said. "Then tried to fight the Philistines without him."

The lamp guttered again. Michal stood up abruptly. "I'm going to get some more oil."

Ishvi nodded. "You—you don't have to wait," he told her. "You can go to bed."

"Of course I want to wait," she answered. "It's my husband."

She meant Paltiel, who'd gone with Abner. But as she swept out she realised that she could have meant David.

The storeroom, where the oil was kept, was at the other end of Ishvi's house. Michal tiptoed out into the central courtyard, past curtained rooms where various others slept. She pushed at the storeroom door and felt around for the cup to dip into one of the big jars. Carefully she poured the thick liquid into the lamp's shallow bowl. The flame at its tip grew in strength, like a sleeping animal being coaxed awake.

The door banged.

Michal jumped, slopping oil down her dark skirt. She

cursed. But the light was still burning and she kept it steady in her hand as she hurried to the main door of the house. It banged again: a heavy fist was beating at it. Only Abner knocked that heavily.

Michal drew back the bolts. Ishvi appeared behind her, and together they gazed at Abner's large, scarred face.

Abner said grimly, "They're good fighters, David's men."

Ishvi drew in his breath. "Do you mean—"

"No, we weren't defeated exactly," answered Abner, shouldering his way past them into the house. "They lost as many men as we did. I killed one of their captains. Asahel was his name. Brother of Joab and Abishai." He smiled briefly. "But it wasn't enough. We won't defeat David that easily."

A thin, sharp sense of triumph curled into Michal. She looked at her brother and snorted: he wore the expression of a child who had been promised a honey cake and then been forced to watch someone else eat it instead.

Abner was looking at Ishvi too—looking him up and down. He was assessing him, Michal realised. Like he was choosing which camel to back in a race.

And judging by the glint in his eye, Ishvi wasn't the camel Abner was going to choose.

Nobody bothered to tell Michal most things, but she kept her eyes and ears open. She watched Abner. She found out who came to his house. She listened at doors. She lingered in rooms she wasn't supposed to be in.

Abner controlled Ishvi completely now. But would he make himself king, or would he go over to David?

And would David take him?

And what about *her*?

She waited. There was nothing else to do.

Eventually Ishvi called her to see him.

She found her brother alone, fiddling with the bottom of his tunic. He looked up at her as if she'd caught him doing something dreadful.

Michal kept her voice cold. "You asked for me?"

His pasty face was round and fearful. "D—David wants you," he said.

So. Michal dug her nails into her palm. That was how it was to be.

"Abner says—Abner says you must go to him," Ishvi wobbled.

Abner.

She saw very clearly what was going on. Abner had decided that David was the camel to back. He had clicked his fingers, and Michal was going to be taken away from Paltiel and Mahanaim and sent south. She was going to be the proof of Abner's power over Ishvi, and of his freshly painted loyalty to David.

Was David really going to be fooled by that? Abner wasn't loyal to anyone. He did what he wanted, and made other people think they'd told him to do it.

"You'll be David's wife again," whispered Ishvi, "and…" But he trailed off, and turned away.

Michal felt a flood of anger. "Coward," she spat. Would he send her away that easily? Would he give up his kingdom that fast? Could he not even look at his own sister's face as she registered the news?

Apparently not.

She stalked out of the room.

CHAPTER 27

King and Queen

The donkey was decked with finery. Gold coins spun on threads sewn into its bridle, and the saddle-cloths were rich and embroidered, with wedges of thick wool to make the seat comfortable. Michal herself, riding it, felt stiff with decoration: the bangles on her wrists and ankles, the complicated headdress folded around her hair… But stiffness was what she needed right now. She had to look, and think, and feel, like a queen.

She hadn't put it all on until they were well into Judah and close to Hebron, the city where David ruled as king. They'd come down through Israel without anyone knowing she was any different than her servant, Noa. They'd even passed through Gibeah, dear old Gibeah, without anyone calling out her name.

Then she'd asked the men to halt, and she and Noa had pulled the finery out of the saddlebags. Silently she'd thanked Ishvi for providing it all: at least he'd got one thing right.

Once Michal had bedecked herself with jewels, and Noa had wound the fine blue cloth around her head, she had climbed carefully back onto her donkey and nodded to Abner that she was ready to go.

"Yes, my lady," he'd answered. Michal couldn't tell whether his smile meant approval or mockery.

She *hated* him.

Paltiel had blubbered and sobbed like a fool. He'd even followed them—Michal and Noa and Abner and the other men: he'd trailed after them all the way to Judah, still weeping. Michal told him he was a fool. What was the point? It had all already been decided.

She, meanwhile, had resolved *not* to make a fool of herself. Saul and Ishvi and soft-hearted Paltiel had all done it, but she wasn't going to. No anger, no coward-ice, no sobbing. She was going to kiss David's hand, and be his queen. That was that.

Noa, on foot beside her, reached out to pat her on the knee. "We're nearly there, love," she said softly. "Are you ready?"

Michal didn't meet her eye. "Of course," she said.

In Hebron you wouldn't have guessed that there had been so much fighting going on for so long. The build-ings were stone and the animals and people looked well-fed, with good teeth and shining hair. There were no beggars at the gate. Somehow the streets didn't seem as full of shadows as they did in the rest of Israel.

David's house was a large one. In a courtyard, tables were set out for a feast; bread and olives and wine were laid out already, and the smell of roasting lamb floated invitingly through a low arch that, Michal thought, must lead to a second courtyard.

A servant ushered Michal and Abner towards another archway. For the first time Michal wondered what all this was like for her father's cousin. He seemed calm—but how dangerous was it for him to come here, really? What would happen if David decided not to trust him after all? The two of them had been enemies for a long, long time.

Maybe David will have him killed, she thought with a small smile.

Then she dismissed the thought with a slight shake of her head. She didn't care either way. She didn't care about anything. She touched the bangles on her wrists, letting them settle neatly, then stepped towards the arch.

It led into a brief passageway. Abner, ahead of her, had to stoop, but Michal held her head high. She couldn't see ahead of him—was it another courtyard they were entering, or a room? Would David be there or—

Abner's great bulk moved out of the way. Michal blinked as her eyes adjusted again to the daylight. Then blinked again. They were in a garden. It was ringed with fruit trees and in the centre a small pool sparkled with water. One corner had a low seat, with a goatskin stretched out above it for shade.

A jug was being pressed into her hands. "Wash—be welcome," said a low voice. David. He was beside her, beaming. Wonderingly she took in the lines that crinkled the skin around his eyes and mouth, the square jaw, the band of gold around his bare head. David! He looked familiar and different all at once. She remembered his face just before he'd disappeared out of the window fourteen years previously. The touch of his hands as he'd tucked her hair behind her ear…

She realised that her mouth was open. Shutting it, she took the jug from David, without touching him. "Thank you," she said.

She plunged the jug into the pool and poured the water over each of her hands, splashing her face too. She wondered how much she had changed in fourteen years. *Too much,* she thought. She noticed that she was trembling.

"I propose to call all Israel together," Abner had begun to say. He sounded casual, almost careless. "I've spoken to the elders already and they are eager to make you their king. The Benjaminites too," he added.

David nodded. "And Ishvi?" he asked.

Abner sneered. "He is nothing. You know they call him Ishbosheth now? *Man of shame.*" He jerked his thumb at Michal. "Look who I've brought. A sign of Ishvi's surrender."

Michal bristled.

But David didn't seem to have noticed Abner's insult. He was holding out his hand. Abner clasped it. The two men embraced like old friends.

David was going to be king of all Israel.

As they went in to the feast, Michal was inwardly seething. Abner—how had he had it all so easy? David was completely taken in, it seemed. No suspicion, no hesitation. He was going to let Abner arrange everything for him, and then make him his commander-in-chief, no doubt. Probably he thought God would always protect him, regardless of how stupidly he acted. What a fool.

They took their places: Michal was next to David. He nudged her as they sat down. "It's been a long time," he whispered, a little shyness in his voice. "It's good to see you."

"You too," answered Michal. "My lord."

After the feast, Abner left and David went off to speak to his advisers. The air was hot. Michal, alone in the garden, settled herself into the seat beneath the goatskin and undid her sandals, stretching out her toes. She could fall asleep here. She yawned. Perhaps she would…

A bang woke her. A man had come through the archway and dropped something on the floor—a sack full of something. It clattered and clinked.

The man was staring at her. His eyes were wild. He wore a dirty, bloodstained tunic underneath leather armour, and his beard was thick and black.

Michal shrank away.

"Who are you?" the man said roughly. "Where's David?"

Michal sat up, remembering herself. "I am Michal, daughter of Saul," she said primly. "And you…?"

The man wiped his brow with a large hand. He smelled, even across the courtyard, of sweat and blood. "Joab," he said. "I have plunder for the king." He kicked the sack at his feet, making its contents jingle again. He was still staring at her. "The son of Saul sent you back?"

"David sent for me." Joab was one of his captains, wasn't he? She'd heard his name hundreds of times. How did he not know of David's plans? "Abner brought me," she added, to see what effect it would have.

"Abner!" The black-bearded man spat on the ground. His eyes narrowed. "And where is that rat now?"

Michal smiled. "The king sent him away in peace."

"In PEACE?" Joab spat again and kicked the sack of plunder, much harder than before. He glared at Michal.

Sweetly, she said, "I think Abner's probably a spy, don't you? A spy for Ishvi. Maybe even for the Philistines." She paused. "He killed your brother, didn't he?"

Joab made no reply. He grunted, grabbed his sack and stormed out of the garden down the passageway.

"David!" she heard him bellow as he went. "DAVID!"

Michal patted her headdress. This was going to be interesting.

CHAPTER 28

Something Sharp

"**A**bner! Friend!"

Abner swallowed his last mouthful of the dried figs that had been laid out for him. He cleared his throat, fixed a smile on his face, and turned towards the man who had just come into the courtyard calling his name.

Joab. His black beard was just like his brother Asahel's.

Abner eyed him warily as he came forward to clap him on the shoulder.

"Welcome," said Joab. "I'm sorry we had to ask you to delay your journey. I hope you hadn't got too far before my messengers reached you?"

"Not too far," replied Abner tonelessly. "What's this about, Joab? I thought I had the go-ahead from the king."

"Yes, yes, David wants you to go and speak to all the elders and get him made king of Israel, that's right. But

227

there's just one more thing... Something very important he wanted me to discuss with you."

Joab's hand was still clasping Abner's shoulder. Abner shook it off. "Can the king not discuss it with me himself?"

"What," laughed Joab, "don't you trust me? I'm David's right-hand man. His business is my business." He looked around. "Now, have you had enough to eat? This is a very delicate matter I need to speak to you about... A private room will be best."

Abner nodded warily. "As you wish."

"This way, then. After you." Joab pointed to a curtained doorway. Abner stumped heavily towards it. He was more tired than he'd thought; he hoped he could get this business done quickly, whatever it was, and be on his way...

The room had a low table and a few rugs on the floor—no chairs or cushions. Abner turned back towards Joab, feeling impatient. "Where—" he began.

But he never finished his question. Joab was close behind him—too close suddenly. His eyes sparkled with triumph. His hairy hand held... held something very, very sharp...

At last Abner realised what was happening. But by then, it was too late.

David and Michal were breakfasting together. At least, David was breakfasting; Michal had finished hers and moved off to the other side of the room, where a loom had been set up for her. She'd only been here two days and she'd woven a hand's-breadth of cloth already.

David was munching, and watching her quick fingers at their threads, and wondering what to say, when the messenger came in and told them that Joab had killed Abner.

Michal stood up, knocking over the stool she'd been sitting on. "Abner's dead?"

David said urgently, "How? When?"

"Joab sent servants after him to bring him back to Hebron," the messenger said. "Abner came back assuming the message was from you. Then Joab stabbed him in the stomach."

David put down his crust of bread. "Where's Joab now? Get him here."

The messenger bowed and left. David stared at the ground for a moment. Then he looked at Michal.

Quietly, she said, "Abner killed Joab's brother, didn't he? Asahel. Your sister Zeruiah's other son."

"Yes." David grimaced. "I should have known it couldn't be this simple."

"But you can still be king of Israel." Michal's face was animated suddenly, her voice urgent. "The elders of all the tribes do want you—I'm sure they do. It'll just take longer to organise without Abner."

He looked at her, amazed. "What?"

"You can still be king, without Abner," she said.

Was that what she thought he'd meant? "No…" he said wearily, sitting down. "I meant, I should have known it wouldn't be simple to… to work with Abner. To bring peace." He put his head in his hands. "I'm not interested in gaining *power*, Michal. I want… I want my kingdom to be one where people act *justly*. Follow God's law. Find it in themselves not to kill each other…"

She looked hurt. "You've killed plenty of people in battle."

"In battle, in battle," David cried, "that's different! We go to fight; we know we might die. But to lure someone away on false pretences and stab him in the *stomach*? When I'd told him he could go in peace?"

Michal was silent. He looked up at her again desperately. "I'm supposed to be God's anointed king, Michal, but I'm weak. If I were the king I should be, then my kingdom—Judah, Israel, whatever—would be perfectly peaceful, prosperous, full of justice. People would follow God's law and treat each other properly. They'd worship God and honour him as they should. But I… I'm *weak*." David felt his face crumple. "I don't know how to make that happen. I don't know how to be the king the people need."

Michal's brow had furrowed slightly: with confusion, or disdain? Maybe both. "No one can be a king like that," she said. "No one."

He didn't reply.

A knock came at the door: the messenger was back. "Joab is here."

"Good." David stood up again, squaring his shoulders. "Bring him into the courtyard. I'll talk to him there. And I want as many people as possible to see it." He strode across the room. "No one is going to think that I ordered this killing."

They marched Abner's body through the city. Joab and his cronies walked in front of it—David gave them no choice—and David himself came behind. They laid him in a stone-cut tomb, and then they knelt and wept beside it.

By the evening most people had gone. Abiathar the priest stayed, of course. Ahimelek. And a number of other men: the ones who loved the Lord the most, and loved David.

He looked at them gravely. "A great man has fallen in Israel today."

They bowed their heads.

"And today," he went on, "though I am the anointed king, I am weak."

Ahimelek raised his head again: he looked worried. David met his eye.

"These sons of Zeruiah are too strong for me," he said simply.

"No, lord—" someone murmured.

"Yes," David insisted. He shrugged. His voice was bitter. "May the Lord repay the evildoer."

It was the only thing he could think of to pray.

CHAPTER 29

The Dance

Three months later the elders of Israel arrived in Hebron. Two from each tribe. One of them was Oren, Jonathan's old friend. He'd grown stout and was richly dressed, but he had the same eager eyes David remembered.

An old man from the tribe of Manasseh spoke first. "We are your own flesh and blood," he said carefully. "In the past, while Saul was king over us, you were the one who led Israel on their military campaigns."

They didn't ask the question: will you lead us again? They just looked at him warily, waiting to see what he would say.

David took in a breath. He'd waited for this moment for a long time. But they had to know—they had to know that being God's king wasn't just about leading people in battle. That was what Saul had thought, more or less. He had been wrong.

"I…" he began, not knowing how to phrase his words.

Then Oren stepped forwards. He gave a little bow. "The Lord said to you, You will shepherd my people Israel, and you will become their ruler." He smiled. "Didn't he?"

As David met Oren's gaze he felt his own face break into a smile—then a chuckle. Was that what the Lord had said? David had to laugh at the image: himself, back on the hills, trying to keep a flock of stubborn, stupid sheep safe. Getting their droppings on his feet and splinters in his hands as he shoved them out of narrow spaces and pulled out thorns and burrs from their coats. Dealing with their foolishness. Coaxing them into better places.

Yes, he thought. *Perhaps it can be like that.*

He nodded slowly. Then Oren clapped his hands, and somebody produced a flask of oil, and they made him king of all Israel.

The first thing he did was to capture a new city to rule from. Hebron was too far south; it was a town of Judah, not a place to rule all twelve tribes from. The new city, Jerusalem, was between Judah and Benjamin, and it had never belonged to any particular tribe. Which meant, David said to himself as he rode into it for the first time, it would be a good place to bring them all together.

He could hardly believe it when messengers from the king of Tyre came to the city, bringing cartloads of fine cedar logs and a dozen carpenters to work them. "We bring gifts to build your palace," the messengers said.

It was a gift: a sign of friendship. It seemed the Tyrians thought Israel, and not the Philistines, held the future.

"Only a year ago they wouldn't even have been able to get through," observed Ahimelek. "With those carts, and all those logs? They'd have been robbed blind and tied up by the side of the road before they'd got half a mile into Israel." He clapped David on the back. "But now... There's peace now. Law. Things are coming together."

"The Lord is king," added the quiet voice of Nathan, the prophet, who'd arrived in Jerusalem the day before.

"The Lord is king," David agreed.

Not long after that, he called for a huge celebration.

"I love you, Lord, my strength!"

The song began with a single voice, the voice of the chief of the singers. It had a clear, simple sound, the kind of sound which made the air go still and the birds listen.

Other voices repeated the words, and the song began to swell and grow like a billow of wind. "I love you, Lord, my strength!"

"The Lord is my rock," sang the leader, "my fortress and my deliverer."

"My God is my rock, in whom I take refuge," surged

the crowd, "my shield and the horn of my salvation, my stronghold."

As the sound grew, David's own heart felt like it was swelling too—swelling so much it might burst out of his chest. Somehow he kept marching. He lifted his own voice.

"I called to the Lord, who is worthy of praise,
and I have been saved from my enemies."

The way that battle had gone, that last battle against the Philistines... It had been like a flood. Years ago, he'd known a place where some villagers had built a dam to trap the waters of a little stream that ran down through the dry hills. They'd cut careful channels to control the flow, and used it to water their crops and their animals. But in the spring a storm came, and the little stream became a river: howling, furious, fast. David had been there when the dam had burst. The water had roared into the air like a pouncing lion, destroying everything. Soon the crops had been flooded and there was no trace of the dam at all.

That was what the battle in the valley had been like, somehow. The Philistines had come up to attack Jerusalem, intent on destroying Israel's new king. They had seemed so strong. But the Lord had broken out against them and they'd fallen like slender stems of new barley, battered by a flood. They were defeated. Thoroughly.

Ever since, David had felt as if everything were new—

everything had been washed clean. The Lord loved him. He knew it deeply, as he'd never known it before. The Lord loved him, had not just chosen him but *loved* and delighted in him! In spite of everything—in spite of all the years of hiding and running, in spite of Ziklag, in spite of Joab—the Lord was looking after David. Not that nothing bad would ever happen, but even when it did, God would be there. David had God's strength. And that meant he could look after Israel.

"Who is God besides the Lord?" he sang. He'd written the words himself, soon after the battle, and taught them to everyone in the city. It was their song as well as his. "Who is the rock except our God?"

"It is God," the crowd roared, "who arms me with strength and keeps my way secure."

The procession wound up through the city, towards a large flat hilltop where no buildings stood. They'd put up a huge tent there. This was going to be a temple—a place of prayer, a place where sacrifices could be made. They'd brought the ark of the Lord, a huge gilded box with a carved seat on top where it was said the presence of the Lord would sometimes settle. It was a kind of throne. It was going to go inside the temple tent.

Everyone was going to know who the *real* king of Israel was.

David breathed in deeply as the song came to an end. He motioned to the musicians. "Let's celebrate," he cried. "The Lord is our king!"

The pipes and drums began, and soon the trumpets joined them. Impulsively, David pulled off his heavy gold-edged robe. Kingly clothes didn't matter on a day like today. They weren't even right. David was a shepherd! A boy! A servant.

Beneath the robe he had on only a kind of ephod, an apron like the ones the priests wore except much simpler and plainer. The skin on his bare arms prickled, but he didn't mind. He laughed and flung his arms out and danced and leaped. He tipped his head back and drank in the air.

Others were dancing with him. "The Lord, the Lord," they chanted. The Lord was their rock. It was all about him!

Michal was waiting for David when he got home.

She wrenched open the door as soon as he touched it, glaring at him. Laughter bubbled out of him; he couldn't help it. Michal's glare deepened. She pulled him in through the door and slammed it behind him.

"How the king of Israel has distinguished himself today!" she hissed. "Going around half-naked! In full view of the serving girls!"

He had a tunic on now; her hands were gripping the fabric so that it tightened painfully underneath his arms. Sobering, he took hold of her hands and pulled them aside gently.

"It was before the Lord," he said.

She folded her arms.

"It was before the Lord," he repeated, growing angry, "who chose *me*, rather than your father, or anyone from his house! I will celebrate before the Lord!"

He paced away, further into the house, kneading his fists against each other. He couldn't tell if he was angry at her or just sad. She didn't understand. She never had. "I will become even more undignified than this," he said to her. "I will be humiliated in my own eyes!"

He turned back to her, willing her to understand what being God's king really meant—and how weak he was, and how kind God was, and how making a fool of himself before the Lord was really the only sensible course of action.

But her eyes were rebellious and angry. She wasn't going to listen.

He gritted his teeth. "When it comes to those servant girls you spoke of," he told her, "by them, I will be held in honour."

Michal's nostrils flared. Her cheeks had grown pink. Squeezing her lips together, she gave a little half-scream of anger, an ugly high-pitched noise deep in her throat. Then she marched away up the cold stone stairs.

CHAPTER 30

Someone Greater

"Nathan," David said to the prophet one day, "it's not right."

"What isn't?"

They were walking out of the temple tent together; they'd been offering sacrifices of thanksgiving to the Lord. From here you could see all the way down the hillside to the newly built walls that encircled Jerusalem. David's palace was nearby, its cedar beams gleaming and polished.

"Here I am," David said, "living in a house of cedar, while the ark of God remains in a tent. That's not how it should be."

They reached the low wall that edged the terrace where the temple tent was pitched, and leaned against it, looking out over the city. The sky was peaceful above them; there was a soft breeze.

"Whatever you have in mind," said Nathan contentedly, "go ahead and do it. The Lord is with you."

David smiled. He turned and leaned the other way, his back against the wall, facing the temple. It was a good tent: the best cloth, the finest ropes, the richest decorations inside. But it was still only a tent. He could see a built temple in his mind's eye: a proper house, a house for God to live in. It would be a magnificent building, rising higher above the ground than anything anyone had ever seen… It would crown Jerusalem's hill, and whenever anyone looked up at it they'd know that there was a God in Israel.

Yes… They'd have to knock down that small building there, and it'd be a huge job to bring all the wood and stone and other materials up the hill, and they'd need an awful lot of workers… But David was sure it could be done.

"I'll talk to the builders," he said, standing up and patting the top of the low wall happily. "I'll talk to them right now."

That night David dreamed of temples. Gold and silver and ivory; carved angels and polished marble floors; rich embroidered fabrics and tall solid columns. The knocking of hammers and chisels, the shouts of workmen… then the sweet smell of incense rising. The Lord in the middle of it all, a cloud around him that crackled with light. People worshipping: thousands and thousands of them. All the people of Israel. All gathered together.

He woke briefly and turned over. He could still hear hammers knocking from his dream. He shook his head, laughing at himself—then frowned.

He could *still* hear knocking.

He flung off his blanket and slipped out of bed, putting his feet into his sandals quickly and tying a robe around himself. He paused to listen. The knocking was coming from downstairs. It was irregular and insistent.

Who would be knocking at the door at this time? What had happened? Mentally David began to run through his list of commanders, thinking who would be the best person to wake if it was news of war... Not Joab or Abishai. Ahimelek could keep his head in a crisis, and his house was the closest. But who had attacked? It couldn't be the Philistines. Surely it couldn't be the Philistines.

He was careful not to make any sound as he ran downstairs. If there was a crisis he'd rather have a clear head to think what to do, on his own, without having to deal with Michal, or anxious servants rushing around lighting lamps.

But he'd thought the time of crisis was over. He'd really thought...

He pulled the door open.

Nathan stood there, his hand still raised to knock. His head was veiled in a cloak. Drops of rain had been caught on the rough fabric; they glistened in the moonlight. The prophet's face was pale and his eyes were excited.

David ushered him in. "What is it?" he whispered. "It's not—?"

"Nothing bad, no," said Nathan hurriedly. "No, it's… I had a dream…"

"Me too." David grinned. "Hold on, let me get a lamp. Are you hungry? I can find some food…"

There was a small oil lamp on the bottom step of the stairs. He fumbled on a shelf for a flint and struck it once, twice against the stone wall. The sparks flew and the lamp's wick fizzed into flame.

"This way," whispered David, and led Nathan towards two stools. He carried the lamp to the store-room—"Sorry, I'm going to have to leave you in the dark a moment—" and found some olives which he shook out of their jar into a clay dish. He poured out a cup of wine and balanced the dish on top of the cup. Then he padded carefully back towards Nathan, cup in one hand and lamp in the other.

The prophet had taken off his cloak and sat there waiting, his hands clasped together tightly.

"Now then," said David, sitting down and handing him the food and drink, "what is it?"

Nathan took a deep breath. "The word of the Lord has come to me," he said. "It's about the temple."

David leaned forwards excitedly. "Go on."

"The Lord doesn't want you to build him a house."

David frowned. He stood up, hands on his hips. "Go on."

"The Lord has never dwelt in a house. He has lived in a tent from the day he brought our people up out of Egypt. He has never asked anyone to build him a house of cedar."

David swallowed. "So he's... he's angry with me? I've done the wrong thing?

Nathan shook his head. "This is what the Lord Almighty says to you," he said: "I took you from the pasture, from tending the flock, and appointed you ruler over my people Israel. I have been with you wherever you have gone, and I have cut off all your enemies from before you."

David nodded, biting his lip. He knew all this—God had been so kind—even when things had seemed like a mess it had all been for good—but what was coming?

"The Lord says: Now I will make your name great, like the names of the greatest men on earth. I will provide a place for my people Israel and will plant them so that they can have a home of their own and no longer be disturbed. Wicked people shall not oppress them anymore, as they did at the beginning and have done ever since I appointed leaders over my people Israel. I will also give you rest from all your enemies."

Nathan took a deep breath.

David sat down. His mouth was open. "Rest from all our enemies," he repeated slowly. "Peace... undisturbed..."

Nathan smiled. "That's not all."

"That's not *all*?"

"The Lord declares to you," the prophet said, "that the Lord himself will establish a house for you. He said: When your days are over and you rest with your ancestors, I will raise up your offspring to succeed you, your own flesh and blood, and I will establish his kingdom. He is the one who will build a house for my Name, and I will establish the throne of his kingdom for ever."

David blinked.

"I will be his father, and he shall be my son," finished the prophet.

David saw that Nathan's hands were shaking; he hadn't drunk any of his wine.

"So you see," Nathan said, "I had to come and tell you."

David nodded. He laughed softly, then drew in his breath again as the words circled around his head.

I will raise up your offspring to succeed you.

I will be his father, and he shall be my son.

I will establish the throne of his kingdom for ever.

David remembered Jonathan, that day he'd handed over his own robe and all his battle gear, after the death of Goliath. His hands had shaken slightly as he'd clasped David's hands. He'd looked solemn and delighted all at the same time. *Even then,* David realised, *he knew that God had chosen me, not him.*

Now, at last, David understood how his friend had felt. God *had* chosen David to be the king—but in the end he was just a stepping stone to somebody else. Someone who'd come later. Someone who'd be called God's son. God's *son!*

A king like me, and not like me, David marvelled. *A king like God himself.*

No weaknesses. No sin. Just perfect godliness. A perfect kingdom.

And this king was going to come from David's family. And he was going to rule for *ever.*

David's face burst into a grin.

He felt very small, and very happy.

Epilogue

A Thousand Years Later

There was a rumour spreading in Israel.

It started in the north, where the tribes of Dan and Naphtali had once had their territory. It swirled around like a powerful wind, gathering strength. It made its way south: down the river, up into the hill country, out into the wilderness. It reached Jerusalem.

People whispered it in the streets and talked of it in the temple courts. Crowds gathered to speak of it, and dispersed. Eyes looked sideways; hands reached upwards. Hope flickered.

Eventually the rumour blew its way into the house of the chief priest, one of the most important men in Jerusalem, in the shape of two under-priests. They hurried along the marble corridor of his residence, their blue and white robes flapping behind them. They bowed low and kissed the chief priest's hand.

"He's come," began the first under-priest, a young man with a high and nervous voice. "The one they're calling the Son of David. He's in Jerusalem."

The chief priest raised an eyebrow.

"It seems he is actually descended from David," added the second under-priest. "Flesh and blood, ha ha, but, um, his immediate family is nothing—nobodies."

"But people are saying he's the promised one, you know, *the* Son of David—"

"—although actually we've heard he claims to be the Son of *God*—"

"—and he has certainly claimed that he can build the temple, you know, afresh—"

"Destroy it and rebuild it in three days, he said—"

The chief priest stood up. The two young men lapsed into frightened silence. In his gold robe and tall hat he towered above them.

"And," he said in a thunderous voice, "the name of this man…?"

The under-priests looked at each other. They swallowed. Then they blurted out the answer in unison.

"His name is Jesus."

Notes

The story of Saul and David is told in two books in the Old Testament called 1 and 2 Samuel. (There's also a shorter version in 1 Chronicles 10 – 29.) I read and re-read those two books as I planned and wrote this one (and read them again, and then again…). I hope that the retelling I've written matches the original Bible account—not only in the events and characters but in the whole spirit of the story.

But that doesn't mean that I've copied everything across exactly. There are bits of the story missing from my version, and bits of the story where the Bible account doesn't tell us much and so I had to use plenty of imagination.

If you've found yourself thinking, "Did that really happen?" or "That can't be true!" then you will probably enjoy this section. In the next few pages, you can find out some of the reasoning behind the decisions I've made, as well as where in the Bible each part of the story comes from. I'd really encourage you to read the original version for yourself and see if you think I've imagined it right!

At the very end you'll also find a Bible-reading plan. If

you really want to put my writing to the test, or if you just loved the story and want to read more, this will guide you through reading the original story in the Bible itself. It's worth reading—there's much more depth to the original version than I could ever have fitted into this one.

A NOTE ON THE TIMELINE

The Bible doesn't give us lots of information about timescale—we don't know how long David was in the wilderness for exactly, or how old Jonathan was when Saul became king. But we are told some things. For example, we know from 1 Samuel 13 v 1 that Saul had been king for three years before the Philistines invaded. And we know from 2 Samuel 5 v 4 that David was 30 years old when he became king of Judah, and that he became king of Israel seven and a half years later. I've worked out my own timeline based on bits of information like this.

CHAPTER ONE

Much later in Jonathan's story, a song describes his skill with the bow (2 Samuel 1 v 22). I think that by the time he was a teenager he must have been pretty good already. The background to this chapter is 1 Samuel 8, in which the Israelites ask for a king, and 1 Samuel 9, in which Saul goes looking for the donkeys. You'll find out more about the search for the donkeys in later chapters!

Oren and the search for the sheep are my inventions, not taken from the Bible account.

CHAPTER TWO

You can read more about the stone Samuel set up, and the battle that happened just before that, in 1 Samuel 7 v 5-13.

The illustration at the start of this chapter shows the word "Ebenezer" written in the Paleo-Hebrew alphabet. This was the writing system used in David's time.

CHAPTER THREE

The assembly at Mizpah is described in 1 Samuel 10 v 17-21.

The ephod was worn by high priests. You can find a description of it in Exodus 28 v 6-30. It seems to have been a sort of very elaborate apron, with straps that went over the shoulders and a waistband. There was also a breastpiece, which is where the Urim and Thummim were kept. The Bible doesn't tell us exactly how the Urim and Thummim worked or what they were, but it seems likely that they were tokens or stones like the ones I've described. What we definitely know is that they were a way of finding out what God wanted and for making decisions.

CHAPTER FOUR

1 Samuel 10 v 21-27 describes Saul hiding and then being made king. You can also read about his search for the donkeys and his original meeting with Samuel in 1 Samuel 9 v 1 – 10 v 16.

CHAPTER FIVE

You can read about the situation in Jabesh Gilead and the messages sent and received by Saul in 1 Samuel 11 v 1-7. In the Bible story, Michal hasn't been mentioned yet (we first hear about her in 1 Samuel 14 v 49), but I decided to imagine this scene from her perspective so that we would start getting to know her early on in the book. She'll have a more important part to play later!

Saul really did just start ploughing fields straight after he'd been made king (1 Samuel 11 v 5). This seems odd, but we need to remember that Israel hadn't ever had a king before. Samuel had set out the rules ("the rights and duties of kingship", 1 Samuel 10 v 25), but even so, I suppose Saul kind of had to make it up as he went along.

CHAPTER SIX

1 Samuel 11 v 8-15 tells the story in this chapter.

In the NIV translation, verse 8 tells us there were 330,000 men in Saul's army. There probably weren't. The word "thousand" (*eleph* in the original Hebrew) was also used to mean "clan"—a group smaller than a tribe but larger than one family. (That's how it's translated in Judges 6 v 15 and 1 Samuel 23 v 23.) When used in relation to a battle, *eleph* can mean a unit of troops (it's translated this way in 1 Samuel 17 v 18)—maybe all the soldiers who came from a particular clan. A unit might have been anything from ten men to 500! So "330,000" probably means 330 *units*—that's at least 3,000 men, and probably lots more than that, but not as much as 330,000. It's still a big army, just not quite as big as that!

CHAPTER SEVEN

This chapter and the next tell the story of 1 Samuel 13 v 1-15. I invented the part about Jonathan telling Saul not to make the sacrifices.

CHAPTER EIGHT

It's not entirely clear in 1 Samuel 13 exactly what Saul did wrong. Samuel says, "You have not kept the command the LORD your God gave you" (v 13). So we know Saul was disobedient—but it's not clear which part of what he did was wrong. It could be that Saul made the sacrifices himself—when only priests were supposed to make sacrifices—and that was his mistake. I think it's more likely that Saul made the sacrifices in the normal way, with a priest doing it. His mistake was that he was supposed to wait, and didn't. That seems to be the main focus in Saul's explanation of what he'd done (v 11-12).

CHAPTER NINE

You can find this part of the story in 1 Samuel 13 v 23 – 14 v 15. The details about no weapons or blacksmiths being available come from 1 Samuel 13 v 19-22.

Oren is an invented name, but the armour-bearer who goes with Jonathan to Michmash was real (we just don't know his name).

Scholars think that Michmash and Geba are modern-day Mukhamas and Jaba, which are about ten miles north of Jerusalem. If you look on a terrain map online, you can see the deep valley that Jonathan and his armour-bearer scrambled into, in between the two villages.

The name "Hebrews" seems to have been used in this period by non-Israelites to describe Israelites.

CHAPTER TEN

Read the original account of this story in 1 Samuel 14 v 16-30. I imagined the fight between Jonathan and the enemy soldier—I'm sure he fought lots of soldiers, but the Bible doesn't specifically describe any fights.

It's worth comparing Jonathan's attitude in this story with Saul's in the scenes at Gilgal. Have a look at 1 Samuel 13 v 11-12 and 14 v 6. Neither Saul nor Jonathan seem like they've got enough manpower to defeat the Philistines—but they respond very differently.

CHAPTER ELEVEN

Leviticus 17 v 10-14 explains why God told the Israelites not to eat blood. Animal blood was used in sacrifices: when a person deserved punishment, an animal would be killed instead. Its blood was shed instead of the person's blood, and then the person could go free. (This pointed towards Jesus, who shed his blood so that we could be forgiven—see Matthew 26 v 28.) It seems that since the shedding of animal blood had such a huge significance, it was to be kept for that one purpose. No animal blood was to be eaten—it was too important for that.

Saul's oath—which was all about himself and his own revenge, and nothing to do with serving God or saving Israel—has led to the soldiers being very, very hungry. That's why they break God's law. Saul blames them, but it's really his fault.

You can read the original story in 1 Samuel 14 v 31-46.

CHAPTER TWELVE

The Philistines very likely wore feathers on their heads. There are some Egyptian carvings that show Philistine soldiers wearing a headdress with tall thin things sticking out from a band around their foreheads. These might be reeds (long thick stalks), but feathers seem more likely. The carvings have no colour, but I've imagined that the Philistines dyed their feathers a deep red. They could have used a dye made from a certain type of sea snail found in that area of the coast. This dye would later be called Tyrian purple and was very expensive.

This part of the story comes from 1 Samuel 17 v 1-30.

CHAPTER THIRTEEN

The story of Samuel's visit to David is told in 1 Samuel 16 v 1-13, and the story of how David started off in Saul's service is told in verses 14-23. We're not told in the Bible account whether David knew that his anointing meant that God had chosen him as king. It seems to me that his later actions make more sense if he doesn't know—or at least if he isn't sure.

The scene in the tent before David goes off to fight Goliath is told in 1 Samuel 17 v 31-39.

CHAPTER FOURTEEN

Read 1 Samuel 17 v 40-51 to see the original account of this story. I didn't include everything that David and Goliath say to each other—but it's worth reading!

CHAPTER FIFTEEN

You can find the original story in 1 Samuel 17 v 52 – 18 v 4.

CHAPTER SIXTEEN

The Bible doesn't tell this scene from Michal or Merab's perspective, but since they're Saul's daughters and one of them has been promised in marriage to David, I wondered what they'd think of it all. You can read the original account in 1 Samuel 18 v 5-9.

The lines of song about the king and victory are based on Psalms 20 and 21. Both these songs were written by David later in his life, but similar songs will have existed before then.

CHAPTER SEVENTEEN

The Bible tells us about several times when Saul tried to kill David. You can read about his plotting in 1 Samuel 18 v 10-30 (which also tells us how David ended up married to Michal and not Merab) and 19 v 1-7. This chapter focuses on the story from 1 Samuel 19 v 8-10.

The song David is composing in this chapter is Psalm 11. The rest of this psalm talks about fleeing danger and it is traditionally thought to have been written by David at this point in his life. I like the idea that he already had some of the song written, and then added the bits about fleeing danger after he escaped from Saul.

CHAPTER EIGHTEEN

One thing I didn't mention in this chapter is that the statue Michal puts in the bed is an idol—a statue of a false god. The Bible doesn't explain why she has such a thing. It's possible that Michal is worshipping false gods instead of the real God. You can read the original story in 1 Samuel 19 v 11-17.

CHAPTER NINETEEN

We're told that Naioth is where Samuel is and that there's "a group of prophets" there. I imagined it as a community where the prophets live together, but that's just my interpretation.

Nathan isn't mentioned in the Bible account at this point and we don't know if he was there. But he was a real person and we will meet him again later!

Turn to 1 Samuel 19 v 18-24 to read the original account.

CHAPTER TWENTY

The scene with Maoz in this chapter is invented, but the scenes with David and Jonathan are true. Read 1 Samuel 20 v 1-42 for the full story.

CHAPTER TWENTY-ONE

The opening to this chapter was inspired by Psalm 63. Have a read and see if you can see why.

I've skipped forward in the story here. The Bible account describes various things that happened while David was in the wilderness. We're not sure exactly how long David lived as an outlaw like this, but it was probably somewhere between five and ten years.

The biggest thing I've missed out is that David got married again while he was living in the wilderness—to several different women. Marrying more than one wife seems to have been quite common in Old Testament times, even though the Bible's overall teaching is that a man should have just one wife (see for example Genesis 2 v 24; Deuteronomy 17 v 17; 1 Timothy 3 v 2). Whenever a man in the Bible has multiple wives, it generally leads to conflict and sadness. This is true in David's life, too—but we don't see that until much later on in 2 Samuel. So I decided to leave out the multiple wives in my retelling of the first part of David's story.

This chapter picks up the story in 1 Samuel 26.

CHAPTER TWENTY-TWO

The Philistines didn't have just one ruler or one capital city. They were a group of five city-states: Ekron, Ashkelon, Ashdod, Gaza and Gath. Gath was the nearest city to Israelite territory. A person from Gath (such as Goliath) was called a Gittite.

The bit of the Bible this chapter is retelling is 1 Samuel

27 v 1-12. I've missed out the fact that David has been to Gath before—right at the beginning of his time in exile. You can read what happened in 1 Samuel 21 v 10-15.

CHAPTER TWENTY-THREE

This part of the story comes from 1 Samuel 28 v 1-2 and 29 v 1-11. I find it quite hard to understand what David's motivations are in this story. Does he want to fight or doesn't he? What is he hoping will happen? Have a read of the original account and see if you agree with the way I've interpreted it.

CHAPTER TWENTY-FOUR

You can read the original version of this chapter in 1 Samuel 30. Saul's failure to destroy the Amalekites is told in 1 Samuel 15. It's quite a grisly story!

CHAPTER TWENTY-FIVE

The story of Saul's death is told twice in 1 and 2 Samuel. 1 Samuel 31 describes it first of all. Then 2 Samuel 1 v 1-16 tells us the scene I've retold here, where David hears the news from the messenger. Interestingly, the two accounts are a bit different to each other. I suspect the messenger was lying.

One important thing I missed out of my retelling is that David had this messenger killed. You can read about this in 2 Samuel 1 v 15-16.

You can read the whole of David's song in 2 Samuel 1 v 19-27. It's very beautiful.

CHAPTER TWENTY-SIX

You can read the full story of Ishvi's kingship and Abner's battle against David's men in 2 Samuel 2 v 2-32.
The story of how Abner transfers his loyalty to David is
told in 2 Samuel 3 v 6-12.

If you read this story you'll see that Michal's brother
is called Ishbosheth, not Ishvi. My assumption is that
Ishvi (mentioned in 1 Samuel 14 v 49) and Ishbosheth
(mentioned here in 2 Samuel) are the same person. Ishbosheth means "man of shame"—so it makes sense to
assume that Ishbosheth is a nickname for Ishvi, something others called him in order to make fun of him.
(To add more confusion, he's also called Eshbaal in
1 Chronicles 8:33!) To keep things simple, I've just
called him Ishvi all the way through.

The Bible doesn't tell us that Ishvi/Ishbosheth sent
money to the Philistines. But it's very likely that he did.
By the end of 1 Samuel, the Philistines had completely
overrun Israel (except the territory of Judah). Ishvi and
Abner recovered the territory, but I think they were
probably still controlled by the Philistines. I think this
for two reasons. Firstly, 2 Samuel 3 v 18 talks about
David rescuing Israel from the Philistines—which
wouldn't be necessary if Ishvi and Abner had already
defeated the Philistines. Secondly (spoiler alert—this
comes up in a later chapter!), 2 Samuel 5 v 17 tells us
that once David became king over Israel, the Philistines
immediately attacked. It seems like they had some claim

over Israel and they wanted to stop David making a claim of his own. Only when David had defeated the Philistines could Israel truly be free.

CHAPTER TWENTY-SEVEN
The story of Michal's return to David is told in 2 Samuel 3 v 12-21. In verses 22-23 Joab returns from battle and finds out that Abner has been sent away in peace.

CHAPTER TWENTY-EIGHT
Read the full story of Abner's death and David's response in 2 Samuel 3 v 24-39.

CHAPTER TWENTY-NINE
The conversation between David and the elders of Israel at the start of this chapter comes from 2 Samuel 5 v 1-3.

You can read about David conquering Jerusalem in 2 Samuel 5 v 6-12. Jerusalem previously belonged to the Jebusites, a completely separate people group who weren't Israelites. After David had conquered and rebuilt it, Jerusalem became the capital of Israel.

You can read about David's final battles against the Philistines in 2 Samuel 5 v 17-25. It's a really good story but I didn't have space to tell the whole thing!

The celebration I've described in this chapter—and Michal's response—comes from 2 Samuel 6 v 14-23. The reason for the celebration is the arrival of the ark of the Lord in the city. This was a large gold-covered wooden chest, made after the Israelites escaped from Egypt. You can read a description of it in Exodus 25 v 1-22. The ark symbolised the Lord's presence among his people; it had a kind of throne on top of it. It had previously been stolen by the Philistines and then returned to Israel (you can read the full story in 1 Samuel 4 v 1-11 and 5 v 1 – 7 v 2). Now it was coming to its permanent home in Jerusalem.

The song David is singing here appears in two places in the Bible—it's Psalm 18, but it also appears in 2 Samuel 22, where we're told that "David sang to the LORD the words of this song when the LORD delivered him from the hand of all his enemies and from the hand of Saul". I assume that means he sang it at this point in the story! I only copied out a few bits of it, but it's worth reading the whole thing. It tells us a lot about David's relationship with God.

I'm sad that Michal responded the way she did. I guess she didn't realise how big God is and how unimpressive people are—even kings and queens.

CHAPTER THIRTY
You can read the full story of this chapter in 2 Samuel 7.

EPILOGUE
There are lots of places in the Bible that tell us that Jesus is the answer to the promise God gave David. For a taster, have a look at the following Bible passages: Luke 1 v 26-38... Matthew 3 v 16-17... Mark 10 v 46-52... Matthew 21 v 1-11... John 2 v 19.

The Whole Story:
Bible-Reading Plan

If you've enjoyed this story, you might like to read the original! Here is a 40-day plan for reading the whole story in the Bible. It includes some passages which I didn't have space for in my version of the story. Those passages are marked with a star.

See if you can find a ten-minute slot at the same time every day—maybe before you go to bed or when you've just woken up. Use that time to read the day's Bible passage and pray to Jesus about it. Don't worry if you don't understand every detail. Just enjoy the story! As you read, try asking yourself these questions:

What is God like in this passage?
How are people responding to God or relating to him?
What kind of king do God's people need?

Then say or write a prayer based on what you've thought about.

Day 1: 1 Samuel 8:1-22* Israel asks for a king

Day 2: 1 Samuel 9:1-24 Saul's search for the donkeys

Day 3: 1 Samuel 9:25 – 10:16 Samuel anoints Saul

Day 4: 1 Samuel 10:17-27 Saul is made king

Day 5: 1 Samuel 11:1-15 The battle at Jabesh Gilead

Day 6: 1 Samuel 12:1-25* Samuel's warnings

Day 7: 1 Samuel 13:1-15 Saul fails to wait

Day 8: 1 Samuel 13:16 – 14:23 Jonathan attacks
        the Philistines

Day 9: 1 Samuel 14:24-52 Jonathan eats honey

Day 10: 1 Samuel 15:1-35* Saul disobeys again

Day 11: 1 Samuel 16:1-23 Samuel anoints David

Day 12: 1 Samuel 17:1-31 David asks about Goliath

Day 13: 1 Samuel 17:32 – 18:5 David kills Goliath

Day 14: 1 Samuel 18:6-30 David gets married

Day 15: 1 Samuel 19:1-24 Saul tries to kill David

Day 16: 1 Samuel 20:1-17 David speaks to Jonathan

Day 17: 1 Samuel 20:18-42 Jonathan's arrows

Day 18: 1 Samuel 21:1 – 22:5* David runs away

Day 19: 1 Samuel 22:6-23* Saul kills the priests

Day 20: 1 Samuel 23:1-29* Saul chases David

Day 21: 1 Samuel 24:1-22* David and Saul in the cave

Day 22: 1 Samuel 25:1-22* David and Nabal

Day 23: 1 Samuel 25:23-44* Abigail saves the day

Day 24: 1 Samuel 26:1-25 David spares Saul's life

Day 25: 1 Samuel 27:1 – 28:2 David in Gath

Day 26: 1 Samuel 28:3-25* Saul consults a medium

Day 27: 1 Samuel 29:1-11 The Philistine army gathers

Day 28: 1 Samuel 30:1-31 David and the
　　　　Amalekite raiders
Day 29: 1 Samuel 31:1-13* The death of Saul
Day 30: 2 Samuel 1:1-27 David hears the news
Day 31: 2 Samuel 2:1-11 David, king of Judah
Day 32: 2 Samuel 2:12 – 3:5* War between Ishvi
　　　　and David
Day 33: 2 Samuel 3:6-21 Abner transfers his loyalty
Day 34: 2 Samuel 3:22-39 Joab kills Abner
Day 35: 2 Samuel 4:1-12 Ishvi is killed
Day 36: 2 Samuel 5:1-16 David, king of Israel
Day 37: 2 Samuel 5:17-25* David defeats
　　　　the Philistines
Day 38: 2 Samuel 6:1-23 David dances before the Lord
Day 39: 2 Samuel 7:1-17 God's promise to David
Day 40: 2 Samuel 7:18-29 David's response

BOOK CLUB

DISCUSSION GUIDE

ON CHAPTERS 1–6

1. Saul and Jonathan both have mixed feelings about Saul becoming king. What is good about Israel having a king? What is not good? Do you think it would make a difference to your answer if someone other than Saul had been chosen instead?

2. Read 1 Samuel 11 v 1-7. What made Saul take action? What made the people obey him? Re-read chapters 5 and 6 of *The Songs of a Warrior*. Do you think the author has done a good job of describing how Saul felt?

ON CHAPTERS 7–11

3. How would you describe the relationship between Jonathan and Saul in these chapters? How does it start off, how does it develop, and what makes it change?

4. Read 1 Samuel 13 v 5-13. (This is the story told in chapters 7 and 8 of *The Songs of a Warrior*.) Why did Samuel say that Saul had acted foolishly? What do you think a "man after [God's] own heart" would be like? What about today—how can we be people after God's own heart?

5. On page 77 Saul wonders, "Where was God's great love for Israel, the people he'd chosen for himself and settled in this land?" What do you think is the answer to this question? How does God show his love for his people in this part of the story?

ON CHAPTERS 12–16

6. Read 1 Samuel 17 v 28, 33 and 42-43, and 18 v 1. What opinions of David do different people have? What is your opinion of David?

7. What would you say are some differences between David and Saul?

8. On page 124 Jonathan wonders whether he feels happy, disappointed, or something else. What has made him happy, and what has made him disappointed? Do you think you would feel the same way if you were in his position?

ON CHAPTERS 17–20

9. Read 1 Samuel 19 v 8-17. What hints, if any, does the Bible give about the characters' motives, desires or fears in this passage? Re-read *The Songs of a Warrior* chapters 17 and 18. What motives, desires and fears has the author given to each character? Can you think of other possible interpretations?

10. On page 159 Samuel says that the Spirit of the Lord is on Saul. What is happening as a result? Have you

spotted anything else that God's Spirit has done so far in the story? What do you think would have happened if God hadn't sent his Spirit to do these things? (If you're stuck, have a look at 1 Samuel 11 v 6; 16 v 13; 19 v 20.)

ON CHAPTERS 21–25

11. On page 171 David is very thirsty, but he says that the Lord is better than water. What do you think he means by that? What precious thing might you choose to say that the Lord is better than?

12. David didn't want to leave Israel, but in the end he did. What were his reasons for and against going? Do you think David made the right decision? What decision would you have made and why?

13. On page 192 Joab says that God has got David into a bit of a mess. Why does he say that? Do you think he's right? If you ever got to feeling this way, how could you remind yourself that God's plans are always good?

ON CHAPTERS 26–30

14. On page 221 we read that Michal "didn't care about anything." Do you think this is true? What words would you use to describe Michal in these last few chapters? If you could have given her some advice, what would it be?

15. In 2 Samuel 5 v 2 David is described as a shepherd over Israel. David also described God as his shepherd. Read Psalm 23. David wrote this psalm. For each verse, can you think of a part of David's story that he might have been thinking of? Can you think of an experience in your own life that could illustrate these verses?

16. Did you like the ending of the story or did it surprise you? Why?

ON THE BOOK AS A WHOLE

17. Can you think of some ways in which David was like Jesus, and some ways in which he was different?

18. What would you say it means to be a good king?

19. For hundreds of years after David died, people looked forward to the coming of the king who'd been promised. They called him the Messiah. What kind of person do you think they were expecting?

20. Christians today should treat Jesus the way Jonathan treated David: we should recognise that Jesus is our true king, and we should put him first instead of our own hopes or ambitions. What do you think it might look like for you to have Jesus as your King? (You could think about the coming week, or the coming year, or even the rest of your life!)

Enjoyed *The Songs of a Warrior?*
Turn the page for a sample of

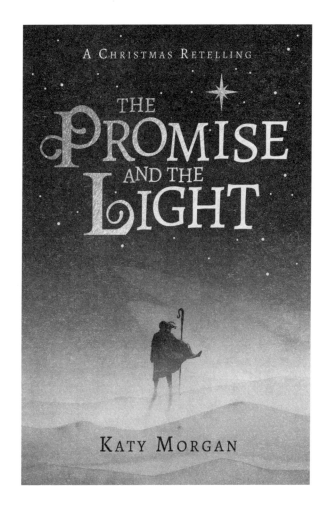

A CHRISTMAS RETELLING

THE
PROMISE
AND THE
LIGHT

KATY MORGAN

CHAPTER 1

The First Moment of the Rest of My Life

Joseph

"Let's go, then," said my brother Josiah as he stowed his tools in the back of the cart. He was scowling impatiently because our father was just sitting there, not moving, not getting ready to head back to Nazareth where we lived, but reminiscing about Bethlehem instead.

"A place to be proud of," he was saying, all misty-eyed. "The city of our ancestors since all the way back before the time of captivity—back even before the time of kings..." He shook his head. "Perhaps I should never have left."

Josiah was glaring at me. Which I suppose was fair enough. It was my fault: I was the one who'd brought up the topic of Bethlehem. I was curious because I'd never been there—and because now it sounded like, before the year was out, I would finally get the chance.

I'd heard the news a few hours before. I was high up on the scaffolding of the half-built bathhouse we were working on, and there was a group of old women talking below. I wasn't paying any attention to them until they all spoke the same word at once.

"Census!"

This sounded interesting. Carefully, slowly, I put down my tools, wincing as the hammer clunked against the planks. But the women below showed no sign of having heard. I leaned out towards them.

It was obvious which of them had brought the news; even from above I could see the gleam of triumph in her eye at being the first to know. "My great-nephew's wife's cousin's friend is high up in the army and he says they're already preparing for it. The Emperor wants to know who is in his empire—a list of names and numbers from every province."

"So he can take more tax off us, I suppose," answered one of the others, and they all muttered angrily.

"But when will this census be, my dear?" asked another. I watched the gleam fade from the first woman's face: she didn't know. "I expect they'll announce it soon," she said, then brightened: "Very soon, if they're making preparations already."

"It'll be chaos," said the woman who had complained about tax. "Hardly anyone still lives in the places their families come from these days. And they'll all have to go back." She seemed rather pleased about this.

Go back to where our families came from! If that was true, it meant we'd have to travel to Bethlehem, my parents and brother and I. All the rest of our family was there—and always had been, for generations, right back to King David himself. I felt excitement rising in me.

But the old women were murmuring again. I knelt down and leaned a bit further out, trying to hear. Why had they dropped their voices? What else were they saying? If I could just get a little closer—and a little bit more—

"Aaargh!" I flailed in the air, losing my balance for a moment, my hands scrabbling to find something to hold onto. Feeling the roughness of wood, I gripped the scaffolding planks with relief and scuffled backwards, breathing heavily.

"That was close." I peered over the edge again. Every one of the old women was fixing me with an angry stare.

"Eavesdropping, boy?"

"No!" I shouted, too loudly, picking up my hammer and waving it at them. "Nearly dropped this! Not eavesdropping! Have a good day, ladies!"

They tutted and moved away. I went back to work. But I was thinking about Bethlehem all the rest of that day.

I'd never been to Bethlehem. I had never travelled anywhere much, really—except to Sepphoris, where we went every day, rattling back and forth in our donkey-cart. We were carpenters, and Sepphoris was a proper town with plenty of building work to be had, not like Nazareth where no one could afford to pay you much for anything. So my father said it was worth the journey. But that was the furthest I ever really had cause to go. Bethlehem seemed almost as far away as the stars.

"I didn't know what I was losing when I left," my father said, still sitting on the donkey-cart and not going anywhere. "Of course, I gained wonderful things… your mother, and the two of you… but I should have taken you back there. We mustn't forget where we come from."

Josiah coughed pointedly, prodding me in the back. He nodded towards Boaz, the donkey, who was standing solidly in front of us. I took the hint: pulling the stick gently out of my father's hand, I struck Boaz on the rump to get him going. Josiah grunted in satisfaction and settled himself down in the back of the cart.

"Do you know why I called that donkey Boaz?" said my father suddenly.

"Yes, Ba—" I said, but it was too late to stop him.

"Not long before our ancestor David was born, the people had no king," he began. "The Lord God raised up leaders here and there, but everyone did whatever they pleased. There was murder, violence—everything was rotten—people stealing from each other, taking advantage of each other, acting with great cruelty—"

"Nothing like today, then," cut in Josiah drily.

My father ignored him. "But in Bethlehem there lived a man of strength and justice. Boaz."

"The great-grandfather of King David," I said.

"A man," Ba went on, "who, when he saw a woman in need, did everything he could to help and protect her."

We all knew the story. He was talking about Ruth: a foreign woman, not one of God's people, who came to Bethlehem poor and almost completely friendless. Boaz helped her, and in the end he married her.

"Boaz and Ruth had a son, Obed," my father continued, while Josiah groaned in irritation behind us, "and their son had a son, and he had a son—well, he had many sons, but the most important was David, who became our people's greatest king."

"We know," said Josiah in a flat voice.

My mother's name was Ruth, too. When Ba first called the donkey Boaz, she had hit him around the head with a cooking pot and told him she'd never felt more insulted. But the name stuck even so. Boaz the donkey was definitely strong, although I'm not sure he was a fine example of virtue and justice. In fact, he was quite lazy.

I raised my stick to tap him across the hindquarters again and he clattered forward reluctantly.

Ba turned to me. "Joseph, it's time you thought about having sons yourself."

"Wha—?" I almost dropped the stick.

"I mean it," my father said. "You're old enough to get married now. I'd like some grandchildren. Some little Davids running around."

Josiah sniggered.

"After all," said Ba, "one day a descendant of King David's will sit on the throne again. Who knows which descendant that'll be?"

My brother spluttered in amazement. "What are you hoping for—that King Herod will adopt one of your *little Davids* and make him the next king?" He laughed scornfully. "Maybe if Joseph has a particularly handsome little son, the Roman Emperor himself will make him his heir."

"Well, of course not—"

"I think we should choose our own king, not sit around waiting for one to appear," declared Josiah. He gazed at the hills ahead of us. Beyond them, I knew, his mind's eye saw Jerusalem, the great city far away in the south.

"That's rebel talk," answered my father sharply. "The king is Herod. And he pays your wages."

Josiah didn't reply. Ba turned back to me. "Is there no one you've thought of?" he asked. "No one you like?"

I could feel my face burning with embarrassment. Of course there was. Of course there was only one person I could ever think of marrying. But I'd never confessed it to anyone.

I took a deep breath. Now was the moment. The first moment of the rest of my life.

"Yes," I said. "I know who I want to marry."

And when I heard what the old women were gossiping about the next day, it was the perfect excuse to go and see her.

the good book
COMPANY

BIBLICAL | RELEVANT | ACCESSIBLE

At The Good Book Company, we are dedicated to helping Christians and local churches grow. We believe that God's growth process always starts with hearing clearly what he has said to us through his timeless word—the Bible.

Ever since we opened our doors in 1991, we have been striving to produce Bible-based resources that bring glory to God. We have grown to become an international provider of user-friendly resources to the Christian community, with believers of all backgrounds and denominations using our books, Bible studies, devotionals, evangelistic resources, and DVD-based courses.

We want to equip ordinary Christians to live for Christ day by day, and churches to grow in their knowledge of God, their love for one another, and the effectiveness of their outreach.

Call us for a discussion of your needs or visit one of our local websites for more information on the resources and services we provide.

Your friends at The Good Book Company

thegoodbook.com | thegoodbook.co.uk
thegoodbook.com.au | thegoodbook.co.nz
thegoodbook.co.in